ALCATRAZ

VERSUS THE KNIGHTS OF CRYSTALLIA

ALCATRAZ

VERSUS THE KNIGHTS OF CRYSTALLIA

BY BRANDON SANDERSON

Scholastic Press ★ New York

Library of Congress Cataloging-in-Publication Data

Sanderson, Brandon.
  Alcatraz versus the Knights of Crystallia / by Brandon Sanderson. — 1st ed.
      p.   cm.
Summary: When Alcatraz and Grandpa Smedry make a pilgrimage to the Free Kingdom city of
Crystallia, they are shocked to find the city under siege by the Evil Librarians — led by Alcatraz's
own mother.
  [1. Fantasy.   2. Mothers—Fiction.   3. Librarians—Fiction.   4. Humorous stories.]   I. Title.
PZ7.S19797A1k 2009
[Fic]—dc22

                                                                              2008049262

ISBN-13: 978-0-439-92555-6
ISBN-10: 0-439-92555-X

              10 9 8 7 6 5 4 3 2 1   09 10 11 12 13

                  Printed in the U.S.A.   23
                  First edition, October 2009

                The text type was set in Minion.
                Book design by Lillie Mear

For Jane, who does her best to keep me looking fashionable, and does it in such an endearing way that I can't even convince myself to wear mismatched socks anymore (except on Thursdays)

AUTHOR'S FOREWORD

I AM AWESOME.

No, REALLY. I'M THE MOST AMAZING PERSON YOU'VE EVER READ ABOUT. OR THAT YOU EVER *WILL* READ ABOUT. THERE'S NOBODY LIKE ME OUT THERE. I'M ALCATRAZ SMEDRY, THE UNBELIEVABLY INCREDIBLE.

IF YOU'VE READ THE PREVIOUS TWO VOLUMES OF MY AUTOBIOGRAPHY (AND I HOPE THAT YOU HAVE, FOR IF YOU HAVEN'T, I WILL MAKE FUN OF YOU LATER ON), YOU MIGHT BE SURPRISED TO HEAR ME BEING SO POSITIVE. I WORKED HARD IN THE OTHER BOOKS TO MAKE YOU HATE ME. I TOLD YOU QUITE BLUNTLY IN THE FIRST BOOK THAT I WAS *NOT A NICE PERSON*, THEN PROCEEDED TO SHOW THAT I WAS A LIAR IN THE SECOND.

I WAS WRONG. I'M AN AMAZING, STUPENDOUS PERSON. I MIGHT BE A LITTLE SELFISH AT TIMES, BUT I'M STILL RATHER INCREDIBLE. I JUST WANTED YOU TO KNOW THAT.

YOU MIGHT REMEMBER FROM THE OTHER TWO BOOKS (ASSUMING YOU WEREN'T TOO DISTRACTED BY HOW AWESOME I AM) THAT THIS SERIES IS BEING PUBLISHED SIMULTANEOUSLY IN THE FREE KINGDOMS AND IN THE HUSHLANDS. THOSE IN THE FREE KINGDOMS — MOKIA, NALHALLA, AND THE LIKE — CAN READ IT FOR WHAT IT REALLY IS, AN AUTOBIOGRAPHICAL WORK THAT EXPLAINS THE TRUTH BEHIND MY RISE TO FAME. IN THE HUSHLANDS — PLACES LIKE THE UNITED

STATES, MEXICO, AND AUSTRALIA — THIS WILL BE PUBLISHED AS A
FANTASY NOVEL TO DISGUISE IT FROM LIBRARIAN AGENTS.

BOTH LANDS NEED THIS BOOK. BOTH LANDS NEED TO UNDERSTAND
THAT I AM NO HERO. THE BEST WAY TO EXPLAIN THIS, I HAVE NOW
DECIDED, IS TO TALK REPEATEDLY ABOUT HOW AWESOME, INCREDIBLE,
AND AMAZING I AM.

YOU'LL UNDERSTAND EVENTUALLY.

ALCATRAZ

★VERSUS★ THE **KNIGHTS**
OF **CRYSTALLIA**

CHAPTER 1

So there I was, hanging upside down underneath a gigantic glass bird, speeding along at a hundred miles an hour above the ocean, in no danger whatsoever.

That's right. I wasn't in any danger. I was more safe at that moment than I'd ever been in my entire life, despite a plummet of several hundred feet looming below me. (Or, well, *above* me, since I was upside down.)

I took a few cautious steps. The oversized boots on my feet had a special type of glass on the bottom, called Grappler's Glass, which let them stick to other things made of glass. That kept me from falling off. (At which point *up* would quickly become *down* as I fell to my death. Gravity is such a punk.)

If you'd seen me, with the wind howling around me and the sea churning below, you may not have agreed that I was safe. But these things — like which direction is up — are relative. You see, I'd grown up as a foster child in the Hushlands: lands controlled by the evil Librarians. They'd carefully watched over me during my childhood, anticipating the day when I'd receive a very special bag of sand from my father.

I'd received the bag. They'd stolen the bag. I'd gotten the bag back. Now I was stuck to the bottom of a giant glass bird. Simple, really. If it doesn't make sense to you, then might I recommend picking up the first two books of a series before you try to read the third one?

Unfortunately, I know that some of you Hushlanders have trouble counting to three. (The Librarian-controlled schools don't want you to be able to manage complex mathematics.) So I've prepared this helpful guide.

Definition of "book one": The best place to start a series. You can identify "book one" by the fact that it has a little "1" on the spine. Smedrys do a happy dance when you read book one first. Entropy shakes its angry fist at you for being clever enough to organize the world.

Definition of "book two": The book you read *after* book one. If you start with book two, I will make fun of you.

(Okay, so I'll make fun of you either way. But honestly, do you want to give me more ammunition?)

Definition of "book three": The worst place, currently, to start a series. If you start here, I will throw things at you.

Definition of "book four": And . . . how'd you manage to start with that one? I haven't even written it yet. (You sneaky time travelers.)

Anyway, if you haven't read book two, you missed out on some very important events. Those include: a trip into the fabled Library of Alexandria, sludge that tastes faintly of bananas, ghostly Librarians that want to suck your soul, giant glass dragons, the tomb of Alcatraz the First, and — most important — a lengthy discussion about belly button lint. By not reading book two, you *also* just forced a large number of people to waste an entire minute reading that recap. I hope you're satisfied.

I clomped along, making my way toward a solitary figure standing near the chest of the bird. Enormous glass wings beat on either side of me, and I passed thick glass bird legs that were curled up and tucked back. Wind howled and slammed against me. The bird — called the

Hawkwind — wasn't quite as majestic as our previous vehicle, a glass dragon called the *Dragonaut*. Still, it had a nice group of compartments inside where one could travel in luxury.

My grandfather, of course, couldn't be bothered with something as normal as waiting *inside* a vehicle. No, he had to cling to the bottom and stare out over the ocean. I fought against the wind as I approached him — and then, suddenly, the wind vanished. I froze in shock, one of my boots locking into place on the bird's glass underside.

Grandpa Smedry jumped, turning. "Rotating Rothfusses!" he exclaimed. "You surprised me, lad!"

"Sorry," I said, walking forward, my boots making a clinking sound each time I unlocked one, took a step, then locked back onto the glass. As always, my grandfather wore a sharp black tuxedo — he thought it made him blend in better in the Hushlands. He was bald except for a tuft of white hair that ran around the back of his head, and he sported an impressively bushy white mustache.

"What happened to the wind?" I asked.

"Hum? Oh, that." My grandfather reached up, tapping the green-specked spectacles he wore. They were Oculatory Lenses, a type of magical glasses that — when activated by an Oculator like Grandpa Smedry or myself — could do some very interesting things. (Those things don't, unfortunately, include forcing lazy readers to go and reread the first couple of books, thereby removing the need for me to explain all of this stuff over and over again.)

"Windstormer's Lenses?" I asked. "I didn't know you could use them like this." I'd had a pair of Windstormer's Lenses, and I'd used them to shoot out jets of wind.

"It takes quite a bit of practice, my boy," Grandpa Smedry said in his boisterous way. "I'm creating a bubble of wind that is shooting out from me in exactly the *opposite* direction of the wind that's pushing against me, thereby negating it all."

"But . . . shouldn't that blow *me* backward as well?"

"What? No, of course not! What makes you think that it would?"

"Uh . . . physics?" I said. (Which you might agree is a rather strange thing to be mentioning while hanging upside down through the use of magical glass boots.)

Grandpa Smedry laughed. "Excellent joke, lad. Excellent." He clasped me on the shoulder. Free Kingdomers like my grandfather tend to be very amused by Librarian concepts like physics, which they find to be utter nonsense. I think that the Free Kingdomers don't give the Librarians enough credit. Physics isn't nonsense — it's just incomplete.

Free Kingdomer magic and technology have their own kind of logic. Take the glass bird. It was driven by something called a silimatic engine, which used different types of sands and glass to propel it. Smedry Talents and Oculator powers were called "magic" in the Free Kingdoms, since only special people could use them. Something that could be used by anyone — such as the silimatic engine or the boots on my feet — was called technology.

The longer I spent with people from the Free Kingdoms, the less I bought that distinction. "Grandfather," I said, "did I ever tell you that I managed to power a pair of Grappler's Glass boots just by touching them?"

"Hum?" Grandpa Smedry said. "What's that?"

"I gave a pair of these boots an extra boost of power," I said. "Just by touching them . . . as if I could act like some kind of battery or energy source."

My grandfather was silent.

"What if that's what we do with the Lenses?" I said, tapping the spectacles on my face. "What if being an Oculator isn't as limited as we think it is? What if we can affect all kinds of glass?"

"You sound like your father, lad," Grandpa Smedry said. "He has a theory relating to exactly what you're talking about."

My father. I glanced upward. Then, eventually, I turned back to Grandpa Smedry. He wore his pair of Windstormer's Lenses, keeping the wind at bay.

"Windstormer's Lenses," I said. "I . . . broke the other pair you gave me."

"Ha!" Grandpa Smedry said. "That's not surprising at all, lad. Your Talent is quite powerful."

My Talent — my Smedry Talent — was the magical ability to break things. Every Smedry has a Talent, even those who are only Smedrys by marriage. My grandfather's Talent was the ability to arrive late to appointments.

The Talents were both blessings and curses. My grandfather's Talent, for instance, was quite useful when he arrived late to things like bullets or tax day. But he'd also arrived too late to stop the Librarians from stealing my inheritance.

Grandpa Smedry fell uncharacteristically silent as he stared out over the ocean, which seemed to hang above us. West. Toward Nalhalla, my homeland, though I'd never once set foot upon its soil.

7

"What's wrong?" I asked.

"Hum? Wrong? Nothing's wrong! Why, we rescued your father from the Curators of Alexandria themselves! You showed a very Smedry-like keenness of mind, I must say. Very well done! We've been victorious!"

"Except for the fact that my mother now has a pair of Translator's Lenses," I said.

"Ah, yes. There *is* that."

The Sands of Rashid, which had started this entire mess, had been forged into Lenses that could translate any language. My father had somehow collected the Sands of Rashid, then he'd split them and sent half to me, enough to forge a single pair of spectacles. He'd kept the other pair for himself. After the fiasco at the Library of Alexandria, my mother had managed to steal his pair. (I still had mine, fortunately.)

Her theft meant that, if she had access to an Oculator, she could read the Forgotten Language and understand the secrets of the ancient Incarna people. She could read about their technological and magical marvels, discovering advanced weapons. This was a problem. You see, my mother was a Librarian.

"What are we going to do?" I asked.

"I'm not sure," Grandpa Smedry said. "But I intend to speak with the Council of Kings. They should have something to say on this, yes indeed." He perked up. "Anyway, there's no use worrying about it at the moment! Surely you didn't come all the way down here just because you wanted to hear doom and gloom from your favorite grandfather!"

I almost replied that he was my *only* grandfather. Then I thought for a moment about what having only one grandfather would imply. Ew.

"Actually," I said, looking up toward the *Hawkwind*, "I wanted to ask you about my father."

"What about him, lad?"

"Has he always been so . . ."

"Distracted?"

I nodded.

Grandpa Smedry sighed. "Your father is a very driven man, Alcatraz. You know that I disapprove of the way he left you to be raised in the Hushlands . . . but, well, he *has* accomplished some great things in his life. Scholars have been trying to crack the Forgotten Language for millennia! I was convinced that it couldn't be done. Beyond that, I don't think any Smedry has mastered their Talent as well as he has."

9

Through the glass above, I could see shadows and shapes — our companions. My father was there, a man I'd spent my entire childhood wondering about. I'd expected him to be a little more . . . well, excited to see me.

Even if he *had* abandoned me in the first place.

Grandpa Smedry rested his hand on my shoulder. "Ah, don't look so glum. Amazing Abrahams, lad! You're about to visit Nalhalla for the first time! We'll work this all out eventually. Sit back and rest for a bit. You've had a busy few months."

"How close are we anyway?" I asked. We'd been flying for the better part of the morning. That was after we'd spent two weeks camped outside the Library of Alexandria, waiting for my uncle Kaz to make his way to Nalhalla and send a ship back to pick us up. (He and Grandpa Smedry had agreed that it would be faster for Kaz to go by himself. Like the rest of us, Kaz's Talent — which is the ability to get lost in very spectacular ways — can be unpredictable.)

"Not too far, I'd say," Grandpa Smedry said, pointing. "Not far at all . . ."

I turned to look across the waters, and there it was. A distant continent, just coming into view. I took a step forward, squinting from my upside-down vantage. There was a city built along the coast of the continent, rising boldly in the early light.

"Castles," I whispered as we approached. "It's filled with castles?"

There were dozens of them, perhaps hundreds. The entire *city* was made of castles, reaching toward the sky, lofty towers and delicate spires. Flags flapping from the very tips. Each castle had a different design and shape, and a majestic city wall surrounded them all.

Three structures dominated the rest. One was a powerful black castle on the far south side of the city. Its sides were sheer and tall, and it had a powerful feel to it, like a mountain. Or a really big stone bodybuilder. In the middle of the city, there was a strange white castle that looked something like a pyramid with towers and parapets. It flew an enormous, brilliant red flag that I could make out even from a distance.

On the far north side of the city, to my right, was the oddest structure of all. It appeared to be a gigantic crystalline mushroom. It was at least a hundred feet tall and twice as wide. It sprouted from the city, its bell top throwing a huge shadow over a bunch of smaller castles. Atop the mushroom sat a more traditional-looking castle that sparkled in the sunlight, as if constructed entirely from glass.

"Crystallia?" I asked, pointing.

"Yes indeed!" Grandpa Smedry said.

Crystallia, home of the Knights of Crystallia, sworn protectors of the Smedry clan and the royalty of the Free Kingdoms. I glanced back up at the *Hawkwind*. Bastille waited inside, still under condemnation for having lost her sword back in the Hushlands. Her homecoming would not be as pleasant as mine would be.

But . . . well, I couldn't focus on that at the moment. I was coming *home*. I wish I could explain to you how it felt to finally see Nalhalla. It wasn't a crazy sense of excitement or glee — it was far more peaceful. Imagine what it's like to wake up in the morning, refreshed and alert after a remarkably good sleep.

It felt *right*. Serene.

That, of course, meant it was time for something to explode.

CHAPTER 2

I hate explosions. Not only are they generally bad for one's health but they're just so demanding. Whenever one comes along, you have to pay attention to it instead of whatever else you were doing. In fact, explosions are suspiciously like baby sisters in that regard.

Fortunately, I'm not going to talk about the *Hawkwind* exploding right now. Instead, I'm going to talk about something completely unrelated: fish sticks. (Get used to it. I do this sort of thing all the time.)

Fish sticks are, without a doubt, the most disgusting things ever created. Regular fish is bad enough, but fish sticks . . . well, they raise disgustingness to an entirely new level. It's like they exist *just* to make us writers come up with new words to describe them, since the old words just aren't horrible enough. I'm thinking of using *crapaflapnasti*.

Definition of "crapaflapnasti": "Adj. Used to describe an item that is as disgusting as fish sticks." (Note: This word can only be used to describe fish sticks themselves, as nothing has yet been found that is equally *crapaflapnasti*. Though the unclean, moldy, cluttered space under Brandon Sanderson's bed comes close.)

Why am I telling you about fish sticks? Well, because in addition to being an unwholesome blight upon the land, they're all pretty much the same. If you don't like one brand, chances are very good you won't like any of them.

The thing is, I've noticed that people tend to treat books like fish sticks. People try one, and they figure they've tried them all.

Books are not fish sticks. While they're not all as awesome as the one you are now holding, there's so much variety to them that it can be unsettling. Even within the same genre, two books can be totally different.

We'll talk more about this later. For now, just try not to treat books like fish sticks. (And if you are forced to eat one of the two, go with the books. Trust me.)

The right side of the *Hawkwind* exploded.

The vehicle pitched in the air, chunks of glass sparkling as they blew free. To the side of me, the glass bird's leg broke off and the world lurched, spun, and distorted — like I was riding a madman's version of a merry-go-round.

At that moment, my panicked mind realized that the section of glass under my feet — the one my boots were still stuck to — had broken away from the *Hawkwind*. The vehicle was still managing to fly. I, however, was not. Unless you count plummeting to your doom at a hundred miles an hour "flying."

Everything was a blur. The large piece of glass I was stuck to was flipping end over end, the wind tossing it about like a sheet of paper. I didn't have much time.

Break! I thought, sending a shock of my Talent through my legs, shattering my boots and the sheet beneath them. Shards of glass exploded around me, but I stopped spinning. I twisted, looking down at the waves. I didn't have any Lenses that could save me — all I was carrying were the Translator's Lenses and my Oculator's Lenses. All my other pairs had been broken, given away, or returned to Grandpa Smedry.

That only left my Talent. The wind whistled about me, and I extended my arms. I always wondered just what my Talent could break, if given the chance. Could I, perhaps . . . I closed my eyes, gathering my power.

BREAK! I thought, shooting the power out of my arms and into the air.

Nothing happened.

I opened my eyes, terrified, as the waves rushed up at me. And rushed up at me. And rushed up at me. And . . . rushed up at me some more.

It sure is taking a long time for me to plunge to my death, I thought. I *felt* as if I were falling, yet the nearby waves didn't actually seem to be getting any closer.

I turned, looking upward. There, falling toward me, was Grandpa Smedry, his tuxedo jacket flapping, a look of intense concentration on his face as he held his hand toward me, fingers extended.

He's making me arrive late to my fall! I thought. On occasion, I'd been able to make my Talent work at a distance, but it was difficult and unpredictable.

"Grandpa!" I yelled in excitement.

Right about that moment, he plowed into me face-first, and both of us crashed into the ocean. The water was cold, and my exclamation of surprise quickly turned into a gurgle.

I burst free from the water, sputtering. Fortunately, the water was calm — if frigid — and the waves weren't bad. I straightened my Lenses — which, remarkably, had remained on my face — and looked around for my grandfather, who came up a few seconds later, his mustache drooping and his wisps of white hair plastered to his otherwise bald head.

"Wasted Westerfields!" he exclaimed. "That was exciting, eh, lad?"

I shivered in response.

"All right, prepare yourself," Grandpa Smedry said. He looked surprisingly fatigued.

"For what?" I asked.

"I'm letting us arrive late to some of that fall, lad," Grandpa Smedry said. "But I can't make it go away entirely. And I don't think I can bear it for long!"

"So, you mean that —" I cut off as it hit me. It was as if I'd landed in the water again, the air getting knocked out of my lungs. I slipped beneath the ocean waters, disoriented and freezing, then forced myself to struggle back up toward the sparkling light. I burst into the air and took a gasping breath.

Then it hit me again. Grandpa Smedry had broken our plummet into small steps, but even those small steps were dangerous. As I sank again, I barely caught sight of my grandfather trying to stay afloat. He wasn't doing any better than I was.

I felt useless — I should have been able to do something with my Talent. Everyone always told me that my ability to break things was powerful — and, indeed, I'd done some amazing things with it. But I still didn't have the control that I envied in Grandpa Smedry or my cousins.

True, I'd only even been aware of my place as a Smedry for about four months. But it's hard to not be down on yourself when you're in the middle of drowning. So I did the sensible thing and went ahead and passed out.

When I awoke, I was — fortunately — not dead, though part of me wished that I was. I hurt pretty much all over, as if I'd been stuffed inside a punching bag, which had then been put through a blender. I groaned, opening my eyes. A slender young woman knelt beside me. She had long silver hair and wore a militaristic uniform.

She looked angry. In other words, she looked just about like she always did. "You did that on *purpose*," Bastille accused.

I sat up, raising a hand to my head. "Yes, Bastille. I keep trying to get killed because it's inconvenient for you."

She eyed me. I could tell that a little piece of her *did* believe that we Smedrys got ourselves into trouble just to make her life difficult.

My jeans and shirt were still wet, and I lay in a puddle of salty seawater, so it probably hadn't been very long since the fall. The sky was open above me, and to my right, the *Hawkwind* stood on its one remaining leg, perched on the side of a wall. I blinked, realizing that I was on top of some kind of castle tower.

"Australia managed to get the *Hawkwind* down to grab you two out of the water," Bastille said, answering my unasked question as she stood up. "We aren't sure what caused the explosion. It came from one of the rooms, that's all we know."

I forced myself to my feet, looking over at the silimatic vehicle. The entire right side had blown out, exposing the rooms inside. One of the wings was laced with cracks, and — as I'd so vividly discovered — a large chunk of the bird's chest had fallen free.

My grandfather was sitting beside the tower's railing, and he waved weakly as I looked over. The others were slowly trying to climb out of the *Hawkwind*. The explosion had destroyed the boarding steps.

"I'll go get help," Bastille said. "Check on your grandfather, and *try* not to fall off the tower's edge or anything while I'm gone." With that, she dashed down a set of steps into the tower.

I walked over to my grandfather. "You all right?"

"Course I am, lad, of course I am." Grandpa Smedry smiled through a sodden mustache. I'd seen him this tired only once before, just after our battle with Blackburn.

"Thanks for saving me," I said, sitting down next to him.

"Just returning the favor," Grandpa Smedry said with a wink. "I believe *you* saved *me* back in that library infiltration."

That had mostly been a matter of luck. I glanced at the *Hawkwind*, where our companions were still trying to find a way down. "I wish I could use my Talent like you use yours."

"What? Alcatraz, you're very good with your Talent. I saw you shatter that glass you were stuck to. I'd never have gotten a line of sight on you in time if you hadn't done that! Your quick thinking saved your life."

"I tried to do more," I said. "But it didn't work."

"More?"

I blushed. It now seemed silly. "I figured . . . well, I thought if I could break gravity, then I could fly."

Grandpa Smedry chuckled quietly. "Break gravity, eh? Very bold of you, very bold. A very Smedry-like attempt! But a little bit beyond the scope of even *your* power, I'd say. Imagine the chaos if gravity stopped working all across the entire world!"

I don't have to imagine it. I've lived it. But, then, we'll get to that. Eventually.

There was a scrambling sound, and a figure finally managed to leap from the broken side of the *Hawkwind* and land on the tower top. Draulin, Bastille's mother, was an austere woman in silvery armor. A full Knight of Crystallia — a title Bastille had recently lost — Draulin was very effective at the things she did. Those included: protecting Smedrys, being displeased by things, and making the rest of us feel like slackers.

Once on the ground, she was able to assist the vehicle's other two occupants. Australia Smedry, my cousin, was a plump, sixteen-year-old Mokian girl. She wore a colorful, single-piece dress that looked something like a sheet and — like her brother — had tan skin and dark hair. (Mokians are relatives of the Hushlands' Polynesian people.) As she hit the floor, she rushed over to Grandpa Smedry and me.

"Oh, Alcatraz!" she said. "Are you all right? I didn't see you fall, I was too busy with the explosion. Did you see it?"

"Um, yes, Australia," I said. "It kind of blew me off of the *Hawkwind*."

"Oh, right," she said, bouncing slightly up and down on her heels. "If Bastille hadn't been watching, we'd have *never* seen where you hit! It didn't hurt too much when I dropped you on the top of the tower here, did it? I had to scoop you up in the *Hawkwind*'s leg and set you down here so that I could land. It's missing a leg now. I don't know if you noticed."

"Yeah," I said tiredly. "Explosion, remember?"

"Of course I remember, silly!"

That's Australia. She's not dim-witted, she just has trouble remembering to be smart.

The last person off the *Hawkwind* was my father, Attica Smedry. He was a tall man with messy hair, and he wore a pair of red-tinted Oculator's Lenses. Somehow, on him, they didn't look pinkish and silly like I always felt they did on me.

He walked over to Grandpa Smedry and me. "Ah, well," he said. "Everyone's all right, I see. That's great."

We watched each other awkwardly for a moment. My father didn't seem to know what else to say, as if made uncomfortable by the need to act parental. He seemed relieved when Bastille charged back up the steps, a veritable fleet of servants following behind, wearing the tunics and trousers that were standard Free Kingdomer garb.

"Ah," my father said. "Excellent! I'm sure the servants will know what to do. Glad you're not hurt, son." He walked quickly toward the stairwell.

"Lord Attica!" one of the servants said. "It's been so long."

"Yes, well, I have returned," my father replied. "I shall require my rooms made up immediately and a bath drawn. Inform the Council of Kings that I will soon be addressing them in regards to a very important matter. Also, let the newspapers know that I'm available for interviews." He hesitated. "Oh, and see to my son. He will need, er, clothing and things like that."

He disappeared down the steps, a pack of servants following him like puppies. "Wait a sec," I said, standing and turning to Australia. "Why are they so quick to obey?"

"They're his servants, silly. That's what they do."

"His servants?" I asked, stepping over to the side of the tower to get a better look at the building below. "Where are we?"

"Keep Smedry, of course," Australia said. "Um . . . where else would we be?"

I looked out over the city, realizing that we had landed the *Hawkwind* on one of the towers of the stout black castle I'd seen earlier. Keep Smedry. "We have our own *castle*?" I asked with shock, turning to my grandfather.

A few minutes of rest had done him some good, and the twinkle was back in his eyes as he stood up, dusting off his soggy tuxedo. "Of course we do, lad! We're Smedrys!"

Smedrys. I still didn't really understand what that meant. For your information, it meant . . . well, I'll explain it in the next chapter. I'm feeling too lazy right now.

One of the servants, a doctor of some sort, began to prod at Grandpa Smedry, looking into his eyes, asking him to count backward. Grandpa looked as if he wanted to escape the treatment, but then noticed Bastille and Draulin standing side by side, arms folded, similarly determined expressions on their faces. Their postures indicated that my grandfather and I *would* be checked over, even if our knights had to string us up by our heels to make it happen.

I sighed, leaning back against the rim of the tower. "Hey, Bastille," I said as some servants brought me and Grandpa Smedry towels.

"What?" she asked, walking over.

"How'd you get down?" I said, nodding to the broken *Hawkwind*. "Everyone else was trapped inside when I woke up."

"I . . ."

"She jumped free!" Australia exclaimed. "Draulin said the glass was precarious and that we should test it, but Bastille jumped right on out!"

Bastille shot Australia a glare, but the Mokian girl kept on talking, oblivious. "She must have been really worried about you, Alcatraz. She ran right over to your side. I —"

Bastille tried, subtly, to stomp on Australia's foot.

"Oh!" Australia said. "We squishing ants?"

Remarkably, Bastille blushed. Was she embarrassed for disobeying her mother? Bastille tried so hard to please the woman, but I was certain that pleasing Draulin was pretty much impossible. I mean, it couldn't have been concern for *me* that made her jump out of the vehicle. I was well aware of how infuriating she found me.

But . . . what if she *was* worried about me? What did that mean? Suddenly, I found myself blushing too.

And now I am going to do everything in my power to distract you from that last paragraph. I really shouldn't have written it. I should have been smart enough to clam up. I should have flexed my mental muscles and stopped thinking at a snail's pace.

Have I mentioned how shellfish I can be sometimes?

At that moment, Sing burst up the stairs, saving Bastille and me from our awkward moment. Sing Sing Smedry, my cousin and Australia's older brother, was an enormous titan of a man. Well over six feet tall, he was rather full-figured. (Which is a nice way of saying he was kinda fat.) The Mokian man had the Smedry Talent for tripping and falling to the ground — which he did the moment he reached the top of the tower.

I swear, I felt the stones themselves shake. Every one of us ducked, looking for danger. Sing's Talent tends to activate when something is about to hurt him. That moment, however, no danger appeared. Sing looked around, then climbed to his feet and rushed over to grab me out of my nervous crouch and give me a suffocating hug.

"Alcatraz!" he exclaimed. He reached out an arm and grabbed Australia, giving her a hug as well. "You guys *have* to read the paper I wrote about Hushlander bartering techniques and advertising methodology! It's so exciting!"

Sing, you see, was an anthropologist. His expertise was Hushland cultures and weaponry, though, fortunately, this time he didn't appear to have any guns strapped to his body. The sad thing is, most people I've met in the Free Kingdoms — particularly my family — *would* consider reading an anthropological study to be exciting. Somebody really needs to introduce them to video games.

Sing finally released us, then turned to Grandpa Smedry and gave a quick bow. "Lord Smedry," he said. "We need to talk. There has been trouble in your absence."

"There's always trouble in my absence," Grandpa Smedry said. "And a fair lot of it when I'm here too. What's it this time?"

"The Librarians have sent an ambassador to the Council of Kings," Sing explained.

"Well," Grandpa Smedry said lightly, "I hope the

ambassador's posterior didn't get hurt *too* much when Brig tossed him out of the city."

"The High King didn't banish the ambassador, my lord," Sing said softly. "In fact, I think they're going to sign a treaty."

"That's impossible!" Bastille cut in. "The High King would never ally with the Librarians!"

"Squire Bastille," Draulin snapped, standing stiffly with her hands behind her back. "Hold your place and do *not* contradict your betters."

Bastille blushed, looking down.

"Sing," Grandpa Smedry said urgently. "This treaty, what does it say about the fighting in Mokia?"

Sing glanced aside. "I . . . well, the treaty would hand Mokia over to the Librarians in exchange for an end to the war."

"Debating Dashners!" Grandpa Smedry exclaimed. "We're late! We need to do something!" He immediately dashed across the rooftop and scrambled down the stairwell.

The rest of us glanced at one another.

"We'll have to act with daring recklessness and an

intense vibrato!" Grandpa Smedry's voice echoed out of the stairwell. "But that's the Smedry way!"

"We should probably follow him," I said.

"Yeah," Sing said, glancing about. "He just gets so excited. Where's Lord Kazan?"

"Isn't he here?" Australia said. "He sent the *Hawkwind* back for us."

Sing shook his head. "Kaz left a few days ago, claiming he'd meet back up with you."

"His Talent must have lost him," Australia said, sighing. "There's no telling where he might be."

"Uh, hello?" Grandpa Smedry's head popped out of the stairwell. "Jabbering Joneses, people! We've got a disaster to avert! Let's get moving!"

"Yes, Lord Smedry," Sing said, waddling over. "But where are we going?"

"Send for a crawly!" the elderly Oculator said. "We need to get to the Council of Kings!"

"But . . . they're in session!"

"All the better," Grandpa Smedry said, raising a hand dramatically. "Our entrance will be much more interesting that way!"

CHAPTER 3

Having royal blood is a really big pain. Trust me, I have some *very* good sources on this. They all agree: Being a king stinks. Royally.

First off, there are the hours. Kings work all of them. If there's an emergency at night, be ready to get up, because you're king. Inconvenient war starting in the middle of the play-offs? Tough. Kings don't get to have vacations, potty breaks, or weekends.

Instead, they get something else: responsibility.

Of all the things in the world that come close to being crapaflapnasti, responsibility is the most terrible. It makes people eat salads instead of candy bars, and makes them go to bed early of their own free choice. When you're about to launch yourself into the air strapped to the back of a rocket-propelled penguin, it's that blasted responsibility that warns you that the flight might not be good for your insurance premiums.

I'm convinced that responsibility is some kind of psychological disease. What else but a brain malfunction would cause someone to go jogging? The problem is, kings need to have responsibility like nothing else. Kings are like deep, never-ending wells of responsibility — and if you don't watch out, you may get tainted by them.

The Smedry clan, fortunately, realized this a number of years back. And so they did something about it.

"We did *what*?" I asked.

"Gave up our kingdom," Grandpa Smedry said happily. "Poof. Gone. Abdicated."

"Why did we do that?"

"For the good of candy bars everywhere," Grandpa Smedry said, eyes twinkling. "They need to be eaten, you see."

"Huh?" I asked. We stood on a large castle balcony, waiting for a "crawly," whatever that was. Sing was with us, along with Bastille and her mother. Australia had stayed behind to run an errand for Grandpa Smedry, and my father had disappeared into his rooms. Apparently, he couldn't be bothered by something as simple as the impending fall of Mokia as a sovereign kingdom.

"Well, let me explain it this way," Grandpa Smedry said, hands behind his back as he looked out over the city. "A number of centuries ago, the people realized that there were just too many kingdoms. Most were only the size of a city, and you could barely go for an afternoon stroll without passing through three or four of them!"

"I hear it was a real pain," Sing agreed. "Every kingdom had its own rules, its own culture, its own laws."

"Then the Librarians started conquering," Grandpa Smedry explained. "The kings realized that they were too easy to pick off. So they began to band together, joining their kingdoms into one, making alliances."

"Often, that involved weddings of one sort or another," Sing added.

"That was during the time of our ancestor King Leavenworth Smedry the Sixth," Grandpa continued. "He decided that it would be better to combine our small kingdom of Smedrious with that of Nalhalla, leaving the Smedrys free of all that bothersome reigning so that we could focus on things that were more important, like fighting the Librarians."

I wasn't sure how to react to that. I was the heir of the line. That meant if our ancestor *hadn't* given up the kingdom, I'd have been directly in line for the throne. It was a little bit like discovering that your lottery ticket was one number away from winning.

"We gave it away," I said. "All of it?"

"Well, not *all* of it," Grandpa Smedry said. "Just the boring parts! We retained a seat on the Council of Kings so that we could still have a hand in politics, and as you can see, we have a nice castle and a large fortune to keep us busy. Plus, we're still nobility."

"So what does that get us?"

"Oh, a number of perks," Grandpa Smedry said. "Call-ahead seating at restaurants, access to the royal stables and the royal silimatic carrier fleet — I believe we've managed to wreck *two* of those in the last month. We're also peer-age — which is a fancy way of saying we can speak in civil disputes, perform marriage ceremonies, arrest criminals, that sort of thing."

"Wait," I said. "I can *marry* people?"

"Sure," Grandpa Smedry said.

"But I'm only thirteen!"

"Well, you couldn't marry *yourself* to anyone. But if

somebody else asked you, you could perform the ceremony. It wouldn't do for the king to have to do all of that himself, you know! Ah, here we are."

I glanced to the side, then jumped as I saw an enormous reptile crawling along the sides of the buildings toward us. Like a spider crawling across the front of a fence.

"Dragon!" I yelled, pointing.

"Brilliant observation, Smedry," Bastille noted from beside me.

I was too alarmed to make an amazing comeback. Fortunately, I'm the author of this book, so I can rewrite history as I feel necessary. Let's try that again.

Ahem.

I glanced to the side, whereupon I noticed a dangerous scaly lizard slithering its way along the sides of the buildings, obviously bent on devouring us all.

"Behold!" I bellowed. "'Tis a foul beast of the netherhells. Stand behind me and I shall slay it!"

"Oh, Alcatraz," Bastille breathed. "Thou art awesomish and manlyish."

"Lo, let it be such," I said.

"Don't be alarmed, lad," Grandpa Smedry said, glancing at the reptile. "That's our ride."

I could see that the wingless, horned creature had a contraption on its back, a little like a gondola. The massive beast defied gravity, clinging to the stone faces of the buildings, kind of like a lizard clinging to a cliff — only this lizard was big enough to swallow a bus. The dragon reached Keep Smedry, then climbed up to our balcony, its claws gripping the stones. I took an involuntary step backward as its enormous serpentine head crested the balcony and looked at us.

"Smedry," it said in a deep voice.

"Hello, Tzoctinatin," Grandpa Smedry said. "We need a ride to the palace, quickly."

"So I have been told. Climb in."

"Wait," I said. "We use dragons as taxis?"

The dragon eyed me, and in that eye I saw a vastness. A deep, swirling depth, colors upon colors, folds upon folds. It made me feel small and meaningless.

"I do not do this of my own will, young Smedry," the beast rumbled.

"How long left on your sentence?" Grandpa Smedry asked.

"Three hundred years," the creature said, turning away. "Three hundred years before they will return my wings so that I may fly again." With that, the creature climbed up the side of the wall a little farther, bringing the gondola basket into view. A walkway unfolded from it, and the others began to climb in.

"What'd he do?" I whispered to Grandpa Smedry.

"Hum? Oh, first-degree maiden munching, I believe. It happened some four centuries back. Tragic story. Watch that first step."

I followed the others into the gondola. There was a well-furnished room inside, complete with comfortable-looking couches. Draulin was the last one in, and she closed the door. Immediately, the dragon began to move — I could tell by looking out the window. However, I couldn't feel the motion. It appeared that no matter which direction the dragon turned or which way was "up," the gondola occupants always had gravity point the same way.

(I was later to learn that this, like many things in the Free Kingdoms, was due to a type of glass — Orientation Glass — that allows one to set a direction that is "down" when you forge it into a box. Thereafter anything inside the box is pulled in that direction, no matter which way the box turns.)

I stood for a long time, watching out the window, which glowed faintly to my eyes because of my Oculator's Lenses. After the chaos of the explosion and my near death, I hadn't really had a chance to contemplate the city. It was amazing. As I'd seen, the entire city was filled with castles. Not just simple brick and stone buildings, but actual *castles*, with high walls and towers, each one different.

Some had a fairy-tale feel, with archways and slender peaks. Others were brutish and no-nonsense, the type of castles you might imagine were ruled over by evil, blood-thirsty warlords. (It should be noted that the Honorable Guild of Evil Warlords has worked very hard to counter the negative stereotype of its members. After several dozen bake sales and charity auctions, someone suggested that they remove the word *evil* from the title of their organization. The suggestion was eventually rejected on account of Gurstak the Ruthless having just ordered a full box of embossed business cards.)

The castles lined the streets like skyscrapers might in a large Hushlander city. I could see people moving on the road below — some in horse-drawn carriages — but our dragon continued to crawl lizardlike across the sides of buildings. The castles were close enough that when he came to a gap between buildings, he could simply stretch across.

"Amazing, isn't it?" Bastille asked. I turned, not having realized that she'd joined me at the window.

"It is," I said.

"It always feels good to get back," Bastille said. "I love how clean everything is. The sparkling glass, the stonework and the carvings."

"I would have thought that coming back would be rough this time," I said. "I mean, you left as a knight, but have to come back as a squire."

She grimaced. "You really have a way with women, Smedry. Anyone ever told you that?"

I blushed. "I just . . . uh . . ." Dang. You know, when I write my memoirs, I'm *totally* going to put a better line right there.

(Too bad I forgot to do that. I really need to pay better attention to my notes.)

"Yeah, whatever," Bastille said, leaning against the window and looking down. "I guess I'm resigned to my punishment."

Not this again, I thought, worried. After losing her sword and being reprimanded by her mother, Bastille had gone through a serious funk. The worst part was that it was my fault. She'd lost her sword because *I'd* broken it while trying to fight off some sentient romance novels. Her mother seemed determined to prove that one mistake made Bastille completely unworthy to be a knight.

"Oh, don't look at me like that," Bastille snapped. "Shattering Glass! Just because I'm resigned to my punishment doesn't mean I'm giving up completely. I still intend to find out who set me up like this."

"You're sure someone did?"

She nodded, eyes narrowing as she grew decidedly vengeful. I was happy that, for once, her wrath didn't seem directed at me.

"The more I've thought about it," she said, "the more the things you said the other week make sense. Why did they assign me — a freshly knighted girl — on such a dangerous mission? Somebody in Crystallia *wanted* me to fail — someone was jealous of how fast I'd achieved knighthood, or wanted to embarrass my mother, or simply wanted to prove that I couldn't succeed."

"That doesn't sound very honorable," I noted. "A Knight of Crystallia wouldn't do something like that, would they?"

"I . . . don't know," Bastille said, glancing toward her mother.

"I find it hard to believe," I said, though I didn't completely believe that. You see, jealousy is an awful lot like farting. Neither is something you like to imagine a brave knight being involved in, but the truth is, knights are just people. They get jealous, they make mistakes, and — yes — they break wind. (Though, of course, knights never use the term "break wind." They prefer the term "bang the cymbals." Guess that's what they get for wearing so much armor.)

Draulin stood at the back of the room, and — for once — wasn't standing in a stiff "parade rest" stance. Instead, she was polishing her enormous crystal sword. Bastille suspected her mother had been the one to set her up, as Draulin was one of the knights who gave out assignments. But why would she send her own daughter on a mission that was obviously too hard for her?

"Something is wrong," Bastille said.

"You mean, aside from the fact that our flying hawk mysteriously exploded?"

She waved an indifferent hand. "The Librarians did that."

"They did?"

"Of course," Bastille said. "They have an ambassador in town and we're going to stop them from taking over Mokia. Hence, they tried to kill us. Once the Librarians try to blow you up a few dozen times, you get used to it."

"Are we sure it was them?" I asked. "One of the rooms exploded, you said. Whose?"

"My mother's," Bastille replied. "We think it might have come from some Detonator's Glass slipped into her pack before she left Nalhalla. She carried that pack all the way through the Library of Alexandria, and it was set to go off when she got back in range of the city."

"Wow. Elaborate."

"That's the Librarians. Anyway, something is bothering my mother. I can tell."

"Maybe she's feeling bad for punishing you so harshly."

Bastille snorted. "Not likely. This is something else, something about the sword. . . ."

She trailed off and didn't seem to have anything else to add. A few moments later, Grandpa Smedry waved me toward him. "Alcatraz!" he said. "Come listen to this!"

My grandfather was sitting with Sing on the couches. I walked over and sat down next to my grandfather, noting how comfortable the couch was. I hadn't seen any other dragons like this one crawling across the walls of the city, so I assumed that the ride was a special privilege.

"Sing, tell my grandson what you've been telling me," Grandpa Smedry said.

"Well, here's the thing," Sing said, leaning forward. "This ambassador sent by the Librarians, she's from the Wardens of the Standard."

"Who?" I asked.

"It's one of the Librarian sects," Sing explained. "Blackburn was from the Order of the Dark Oculators, while the assassin you faced in the Library of Alexandria was from the Order of the Scrivener's Bones. The Wardens of the Standard have always claimed to be the most kindly of the Librarians."

"Kindly Librarians? That seems like an oxymoron."

"It's also an act," Grandpa Smedry said. "The whole order is founded on the idea of *looking* innocent; they're really the deadliest snakes in the lot. The Wardens maintain most of the Hushlander libraries. They pretend that because they're only a bunch of bureaucrats, they're not dangerous like the Dark Oculators or the Order of the Shattered Lens."

"Well, act or not," Sing replied, "they're the only Librarians who have ever made any kind of effort to work *with* the Free Kingdoms, rather than just trying to conquer us. This ambassador has convinced the Council of Kings that she is serious."

I listened, interested, but not quite sure why my grandfather wanted me to know this. I'm a rather awesome person (have I mentioned that?) but I'm really not that great at politics. It's one of the three things I've no experience whatsoever doing, the other two being writing books and atmospheric rocket-propelled penguin riding. (Stupid responsibility.)

"So . . . what does this have to do with me?" I asked.

"Everything, lad, everything!" Grandpa Smedry pointed at me. "We're Smedrys. When we gave up our kingdom, we took an oath to watch over *all* of the Free Kingdoms. We're the guardians of civilization!"

"But wouldn't it be good if the kings make peace with the Librarians?"

Sing looked pained. "Alcatraz, to do so, they would give up *Mokia*, my homeland! It would get folded into the Hushlands, and a generation or two from now, the Mokians wouldn't even *remember* being free. My people can't continue to fight the Librarians without the support of the other Free Kingdoms. We're too small on our own."

"The Librarians won't keep their promise of peace," Grandpa Smedry said. "They've wanted Mokia badly for years now — I still don't know why they're so focused on it, as opposed to other kingdoms. Either way, taking over Mokia will put them one step closer to controlling the entire world. Manhandling Moons! Do you really think we can just give away an entire kingdom like that?"

I looked at Sing. The oversized anthropologist and his sister had become very dear to me over the last few months. They were earnest and fiercely loyal, and Sing had believed in me even when I'd tried to push him away. And for that, I wanted to do whatever I could to help him.

"No," I said. "You're right, we can't let that happen. We've *got* to stop it."

Grandpa Smedry smiled, laying a hand on my shoulder. It might not seem like much, but this was a drastic turning point for me. It was the first time I really decided that I was *in*. I'd entered the Library of Alexandria only because I'd been chased by a monster. I'd only gone into Blackburn's lair because Grandpa Smedry had urged me on.

This was different. I understood then why my grand-father had called me over. He wanted me to be part of this — not just a kid who tags along, but a full participant.

Something tells me I'd have been much better off hiding in my room. Responsibility. It's the opposite of selfishness. I wish I'd known where it would get me. But this was before my betrayal and before I went blind.

Through one of the windows, I could see that the dragon had begun to descend. A moment later, the gondola settled against the ground.

We had arrived.

CHAPTER 4

All right, I understand. You're confused. Don't feel ashamed; it happens to everyone once in a while. (Except me, of course.)

Having read the previous two books of my autobiography (as I'm *sure* by now you have), you know that I'm generally down on myself. I've told you that I'm a liar, a sadist, and a terrible person. And yet now, in this volume, I've started talking about my awesomeness. Have I really changed my mind? Have I actually decided that I am a hero? Am I wearing kitty-cat socks right now?

No. (The socks have dolphins on them.)

I've realized something. By being so hard on myself in the previous books, I *sounded* like I was being humble. Readers assumed that because I said I was a terrible person, I must — indeed — be a saint.

Honestly, are you people determined to drive me insane? Why can't you just *listen* to what I tell you?

Anyway, I've come to the conclusion that the only way to convince you readers that I'm a terrible person is to *show* you how arrogant and self-centered I am. I'll do this by talking about my virtues. Incessantly. All the time. Until you're completely sick of hearing about my superiority.

Maybe then you'll understand.

The royal palace of Nalhalla turned out to be the white, pyramid-like castle at the center of the city. I stepped from the gondola, trying not to gawk as I gazed up at the magnificent building. The stonework was carved up as high as I could see.

"Forward!" Grandpa Smedry said, rushing up the steps like a general running into battle. He's remarkably spry for a person who is always late to everything.

I glanced at Bastille, who looked kind of sick. "I think I'll wait outside," she said.

"You're going in," Draulin snapped, walking up the steps, her armor clinking.

I frowned. Usually, Draulin was very keen on making Bastille wait outside, since a mere "squire" shouldn't be involved in important issues. Why insist that she enter the palace? I shot Bastille a questioning glance, but she just grimaced. So I rushed to catch up to my grandfather and Sing.

"...afraid I can't tell you much more, Lord Smedry," Sing was saying. "Folsom is the one who has been keeping track of the Council of Kings in your absence."

"Ah, yes," Grandpa Smedry said. "He'll be here, I assume?"

"He should be!" Sing said.

"Another cousin?" I asked.

Grandpa Smedry nodded. "Quentin's elder brother, son of my daughter, Pattywagon. Folsom's a fine lad! Brig had his eye on the boy for quite some time to marry one of his daughters, I believe."

"Brig?" I asked.

"King Dartmoor," Sing said.

Dartmoor. "Wait," I said. "That's a prison, isn't it? Dartmoor?" (I know my prisons, as you might guess.)

"Indeed, lad," Grandpa Smedry said.

"Doesn't that mean he's related to us?"

It was a stupid question. Fortunately, I knew I'd be writing my memoirs and understood that a lot of people might be confused about this point. Therefore, using my powers of awesomosity, I asked this stupid-*sounding* question in order to lay the groundwork for my book series.

I hope you appreciate the sacrifice.

"No," Grandpa Smedry said. "A prison name doesn't necessarily mean that someone is a Smedry. The king's family is traditional, like ours, and they tend to use names of famous historical people over and over. The Librarians then named prisons after those same famous historical people to discredit them."

"Oh, right," I said.

Something about that thought bothered me, but I couldn't quite put my finger on it. Probably because the thought was inside my head, and so "putting my finger on it" would have required sticking said finger through my skull, which sounds kind of painful.

Besides, the beauty of the hallway beyond those doors stopped me flat and cast all thoughts from my mind.

I'm no poet. Anytime I try to write poetry, it comes out as insults. I probably should have been a rapper, or at least a politician. Regardless, I sometimes find it hard to express beauty through words.

Suffice it to say that the enormous hallway stunned me,

even after seeing a city full of castles, even after being carried on a dragon's back. The hallway was big. It was white. It was lined with what appeared to be pictures, but there was nothing in the frames. Other than glass.

Different kinds of glass, I realized as we walked down the magnificent hallway. *Here, the glass* is *the art!* Indeed, each framed piece of glass was a different color. Plaques at the top listed the types of glass. I recognized some, and most of them glowed faintly. I was wearing my Oculator's Lenses, which allowed me to see auras of powerful glass.

In a Hushlander palace, the kings showed off their gold and their silver. Here, the kings showed off their rare and expensive pieces of glass.

I watched in wonder, wishing Sing and Grandpa Smedry weren't rushing so quickly. We eventually turned through a set of doors and entered a long rectangular chamber filled with elevated seats on both the right and the left. Most of these were filled with people who quietly watched the proceedings below.

In the center of the room sat a broad table at which were seated about two dozen men and women wearing rich clothing of many exotic designs. I spotted King Dartmoor immediately. He was sitting on an elevated chair at the end of the table. Clothed in regal blue-and-gold robes, he wore a full red beard, and my Oculator's Lenses — which sometimes enhanced the images of people and places I looked at — made him seem slightly *taller* than he really was. More noble, larger than life.

I stopped in the doorway. I'd never been in the presence of royalty before, and —

"Leavenworth *Smedry*!" a vivacious feminine voice squealed. "You rascal! You're back!"

The entire room seemed to turn as one, looking at a full-figured (remember what that means?) woman who leaped from her chair and barreled toward my grandfather. She had short blond hair and an excited expression.

I believe that's the first time I ever saw a hint of fear in my grandfather's eyes. The woman proceeded to grab the diminutive Oculator in a hug. Then she saw me.

"Is this Alcatraz?" she demanded. "Shattering Glass, boy, does your mouth always hang open like that?"

I shut my mouth.

"Lad," Grandpa Smedry said as the woman finally released him. "This is your aunt, Pattywagon Smedry. My daughter, Quentin's mother."

"Excuse me," a voice called from the floor below. I blushed, realizing that the monarchs were watching us. "Lady Smedry," King Dartmoor said in a booming voice, "is it *requisite* that you disrupt these proceedings?"

"Sorry, Your Majesty," she called down. "But these fellows are a lot more exciting than you are!"

Grandpa Smedry sighed, then whispered to me, "Do you want to take a guess at her Smedry Talent?"

"Causing disruptions?" I whispered back.

"Close," Grandpa Smedry said. "She can say inappropriate things at awkward moments."

That seemed to fit.

"Oh, don't give me that look," she said, wagging her finger at the king. "You can't tell me you're not excited to see them back too."

The king sighed. "We will take a recess of one hour for family reunions. Lord Smedry, did you return with your long-lost grandson, as reports indicated you might?"

"Indeed I did!" Grandpa Smedry proclaimed. "Not only that but we also brought a pair of the fabled Translator's Lenses, smelted from the Sands of Rashid themselves!"

This prompted a reaction in the crowd, and murmuring began immediately. One small contingent of men and women sitting directly across from us did not seem pleased to see Grandpa Smedry. Instead of tunics or robes, the members of this group wore suits — the men with bow ties, the women with shawls. Many wore glasses, which had horned rims.

Librarians.

The room grew chaotic as the audience members began to stand, producing an excited buzz, almost like a thousand hornets had suddenly been released. My aunt Patty began to speak animatedly with her father, demanding the details of his time in the Hushlands. Her voice managed to carry out over the noise of the crowd, though she didn't appear to be yelling. That's just how she was.

"Alcatraz?"

I glanced to the side, where Bastille stood shuffling uncomfortably. "Yeah?" I said.

"This . . . might be an appropriate place to mention something."

"Wait," I said, growing nervous. "Look, the king's coming up this way!"

"Of course he is," Bastille said. "He wants to see his family."

"Of course. He wants to . . . Wait, *what*?"

At that moment, King Dartmoor stepped up to us. Grandpa Smedry and the others bowed to him — even Patty — so I did the same. Then the king kissed Draulin.

That's right. He *kissed* her. I watched with shock, and not just because I'd never imagined that anyone would want to kiss Draulin. (Seemed a little like kissing an alligator.)

And if Draulin was the king's wife, that meant . . .

"You're a princess!" I said, pointing an accusing finger at Bastille.

She grimaced. "Yeah, kind of."

"How can you 'kind of' be a princess?"

"Well, I can't inherit the throne," she said. "I renounced claim on it when I joined the Knights of Crystallia. Vow of poverty and all that."

The crowd milled about us, some exiting the room, others stopping — oddly — to gawk at my grandfather and me.

I should have realized that Bastille was royalty. Prison names. She has one, but her mother doesn't. That was an easy indication that her father's family was of an important breed. Besides, stories such as this one *always* have at least one hidden member of royalty among the core cast. It's, like, some kind of union mandate or something.

I had several options at this point. Fortunately, I chose the one that didn't make me look like a total dork.

"That's *awesome!*" I exclaimed.

Bastille blinked. "You're not mad at me for hiding it?"

I shrugged. "Bastille, I'm some kind of freaky noble thing myself. Why should it matter if you are too? Besides, it's not like you were lying or anything. You just don't like to talk about yourself."

Brace yourselves. Something very, very strange is about to happen. Stranger than talking dinosaurs. Stranger than glass birds. Stranger, even, than my analogies to fish sticks.

Bastille got teary eyed. Then she hugged me.

Girls, might I make a suggestion at this point? Don't go around hugging people without warning. To many of us (a number somewhere near half), this is akin to pouring an entire bottle of seventeen-alarm hot sauce in our mouths.

I believe that at this point in the story, I made several very interesting and incoherent noises, followed — perhaps — by a blank expression and then some numb-faced drooling.

Someone was talking. ". . . I cannot interfere with the rules of Crystallia, Bastille."

I fuzzed back into consciousness. Bastille had released me from her unprovoked, unregistered hug and moved on to speak with her father. The room had cleared out considerably, though there was still a number of people standing at the perimeter of the room, curiously watching our little group.

"I know, Father," Bastille said. "I must face their reprimand, as is my duty to the order."

"That's my girl," the king said, laying a hand on her shoulder. "But don't take what they say *too* harshly. The world is far less intense a place than the knights sometimes make it out to be."

Draulin raised her eyebrow at this. Looking at them — the king in his blue-and-gold robes, Draulin in her silvery armor — they actually seemed to *fit* together.

I still felt sorry for Bastille. *No wonder she's so uptight*, I thought. *Royalty on one side, hard-line knight on the other.* That would be like trying to grow up pressed between two boulders.

"Brig," Grandpa Smedry said. "We need to speak about what the Council is planning to do."

The king turned. "You're too late, I'm afraid, Leavenworth. Our minds are all but made up. You'll have your vote, but I doubt it will make a difference."

"How could you even consider giving up Mokia?" Grandpa Smedry asked.

"To save lives, my friend." The king spoke the words in a wearied voice, and I could almost *see* the burdens he was carrying. "It is not a pleasant choice to make, but if it stops the war . . ."

"You can't honestly expect them to keep their promises. Highlighting Heinleins, man! This is insanity."

The king shook his head. "I will not be the king who was offered peace and who passed it by, Leavenworth. I will not be a warmonger. If there is a chance at reconciliation . . . But we should speak of this someplace outside the public eye. Let us retire to my sitting room."

My grandfather nodded curtly, then stepped to the side and waved me over. "What do you think?" he asked quietly as I approached.

I shrugged. "He seems sincere."

"Brig is nothing if not sincere," Grandpa Smedry whispered. "He is a passionate man; those Librarians must have done some clever talking to bring him to this point. Still, he's not the only vote on the Council."

"But he's the king, isn't he?"

"He's the High King," Grandpa Smedry said, raising a finger. "He is our foremost leader, but Nalhalla isn't the only kingdom in our coalition. There are thirteen kings, queens, and dignitaries like myself who sit on that Council. If we can persuade enough of them to vote against this treaty, then we might be able to kill it."

I nodded. "What can I do to help?" Mokia *couldn't* fall. I would see that it didn't.

"I'll speak with Brig," Grandpa Smedry said. "You go see if you can track down your cousin Folsom. I put him in charge of Smedry affairs here in Nalhalla. He might have some insight about this whole mess."

"Okay."

Grandpa Smedry fished in one of the pockets of his tuxedo jacket. "Here, you might want this back." He held out a single Lens with no coloring or tint to it. It glowed radiantly to my Oculator's eyes, more powerfully than any I'd ever seen except for the Translator's Lenses.

I'd almost forgotten about it. I'd discovered the Lens in the Library of Alexandria at the tomb of Alcatraz the First, but hadn't been able to determine what it did. I'd given it over to my grandfather for inspection.

"Did you figure out what it does?" I asked, taking it from him.

He nodded eagerly. "There were lots of tests I had to do. I meant to tell you yesterday but, well . . ."

"You're late."

"Exactly!" Grandpa Smedry said. "Anyway, this is a very useful Lens. Useful indeed. Almost mythical. Couldn't believe it myself, had to test the thing three times before I was convinced."

I grew excited, imagining the Lens summoning the spirits of the dead to fight at my side. Or, instead, perhaps it would make people explode in a wave of red smoke if I focused it on them. Red smoke rocks.

"So what does it do?"

"It allows you to see when someone is telling the truth."

That wasn't exactly what I'd been expecting.

"Yes," Grandpa Smedry said. "A Truthfinder's Lens. I never thought I'd hold one myself. Quite remarkable!"

"I . . . don't suppose it makes people explode when they tell lies?"

"Afraid not, lad."

"No red smoke?"

"No red smoke."

I sighed and tucked the Lens away anyway. It did seem useful, though after discovering it hidden in the tomb, I'd really been hoping for some kind of weapon.

"Don't look so glum, lad," Grandpa Smedry said. "I don't think you understand the gem you hold in your pocket. That Lens could prove extremely useful to you over the next few days. Keep it close."

I nodded. "I don't suppose you have another pair of Firebringer's Lenses you could loan me?"

He chuckled. "Didn't do enough damage with the last pair, eh? I don't have any more of those, but . . . here, let me see." He fished around inside his tuxedo jacket again. "Ah!" he said, whipping out a pair of Lenses. They glowed with a modest light and had a violet tint.

That's right, violet. I wondered if the people who forge Oculatory Lenses *try* to make us all look like pansies, or if that was just accidental.

"What are they?" I asked.

"Disguiser's Lenses," Grandpa Smedry said. "Put them on, focus on the image of someone in your head, and the Lenses will disguise you to look like that person."

It seemed pretty cool. I took the Lenses appreciatively. "Can they make me look like other things? Like, say, a rock?"

"I guess," Grandpa Smedry said. "Though that rock would have to be wearing glasses. The Lenses appear in any disguise you use."

That made them less powerful, but I figured I'd come up with a way to use them. "Thanks," I said.

"I might have some other offensive Lenses I can dig up later when I get back to the keep," Grandpa Smedry said. "I suspect that we'll deliberate here for another two or three hours before adjourning until the vote this evening. It's about ten right now; let's meet back at Keep Smedry in three hours to share information, all right?"

"All right."

Grandpa Smedry winked at me. "See you this afternoon, then. If you break anything important, be sure to blame it on Draulin! It'll be good for her."

I nodded, and we parted ways.

CHAPTER 5

It's time for me to talk about someone other than myself. Please don't be too heartbroken; once in a while, we need to discuss somebody who is not quite as charming, intelligent, or impressive as I am.

That's right, it's time to talk about you.

Occasionally, while infiltrating the Hushlands, I run across enterprising young people who want to resist Librarian control of their country. You ask me what you can do to fight. Well, I have three answers for you.

First, make sure you buy lots and lots and lots of copies of my books. There are plenty of uses for them (I'll discuss this in a bit) and for every one you buy, we donate money to the Alcatraz Smedry Wildlife Fund for Buying Alcatraz Smedry Cool Stuff.

The second thing you can do isn't quite as awesome, but it's still good. You can *read*.

Librarians control their world via information. Grandpa Smedry says that information is a far better weapon than any sword or Oculatory Lens, and I'm beginning to think he might be right. (Though the kitten chain saw I discussed in book two is a close second.)

The best way to fight the Librarians is to read a lot of books. Everything you can get your hands on. Then do the third thing I'm going to tell you about.

Buy lots of copies of my books.

Oh, wait. Did I already mention that? Well, then, there are *four* things you can do. But this intro is already too long. I'll tell you about the last one later. Know, however, that it involves popcorn.

"Okay," I said, turning to Bastille. "How do I find this Folsom guy?"

"I don't know," she said flatly, pointing. "Maybe ask his *mom*, who is standing right there?"

Oh, right, I thought. *Quentin's brother, that makes Pattywagon his mother.*

She was talking animatedly (which is how she always talks) with Sing. I waved to Bastille, but she hesitated.

"What?" I asked.

"My mission is officially over," she said, grimacing and

glancing toward Draulin. "I need to report at Crystallia." Draulin had made her way toward the exit of the room, and she was regarding Bastille in that way of hers that was somehow both insistent and patient.

"What about your father?" I said, glancing in the direction he and Grandpa Smedry had disappeared. "He barely got time to see you two."

"The kingdom takes precedence over everything else."

That sounded like a rehearsed line to me. Probably something Bastille had heard a lot when growing up.

"Okay," I said. "Well, uh, I'll see you, then."

"Yeah."

I braced myself for another hug (known in the industry as a "teenage boy forced reboot") but she just stood there, then cursed under her breath and hurried out after her mother. I was left trying to figure out just when things between us had grown so awkward.

(I was tempted to think back on all the good times we had spent together. Bastille smacking me in the face with her handbag. Bastille kicking me in the chest. Bastille making fun of something dumb I'd said. I would probably have a good case for abuse if I hadn't also (1) broken her sword, (2) kicked her first, and (3) been so awesome.)

Feeling strangely abandoned, I stepped up to my aunt Patty.

"You done being affectionate with the young knight there?" she asked me. "Cute thing, isn't she?"

"What's this?" Sing said. "Did I miss something?"

"Urk!" I said, blushing. "No, nothing!"

"I'm sure," Patty said, winking at me.

"Look, I need to find your son Folsom!"

"Hum. Whatcha need him for?"

"Important Smedry business."

"Well, it's a good thing I'm an important Smedry, then, isn't it!"

She had me there. "Grandpa wants me to ask about what the Librarians have been doing in town since he left."

"Well, why didn't you say so?" Patty said.

"Because . . . well, I . . ."

"Slowness of thought," Patty said consolingly. "It's okay, hon. Your father isn't all that bright either. Well, let's go find Folsom, then! See ya, Sing!"

I reached for Sing, hoping he wouldn't abandon me to this awful woman, but he had already turned to go with some other people, and Patty had me by the arm.

I should stop and note here that in the years since that

day, I've grown rather fond of Aunt Pattywagon. This statement has nothing at all to do with the fact that she threatened to toss me out a window if I didn't include it.

The mountainous woman pulled me from the room and down the hallway. Soon we were standing in the sunlight on the front steps outside as Patty sent one of the serving men to fetch transportation.

"You know," I said, "if you tell me where Folsom is, I could just go find him on my own. No need to —"

"He's out and about on very important business," Patty said. "I'll have to lead you. I can't tell you. You see, as a Librarian expert, he's been put in charge of a recent defection."

"Defection?"

"Yes," she said. "You know, a foreign agent who decides to join the other side? A Librarian fled her homeland and joined the Free Kingdoms. My son is in charge of helping her grow accustomed to life here. Ah, here's our ride!"

I turned, half expecting another dragon, but apparently we two didn't warrant a full-size dragon this time. Instead, a coachman rode up with an open-topped carriage pulled by rather mundane horses.

"Horses?" I said.

"Of course," Patty said, climbing into the carriage. "What were you expecting? A . . . what is it you call them? A pottlemobile?"

"Automobile," I said, joining her. "No, I wasn't expecting one of those. Horses just seem so . . . rustic."

"Rustic?" she said as the coachman urged his beasts into motion. "Why, they're far more advanced than those bottlemobiles you Hushlanders use!"

It's a common belief in the Free Kingdoms that everything they have is more advanced than what we backward Hushlanders use. For instance, they like to say that swords are more advanced than guns. This may sound ridiculous until you realize their swords are magical and are, indeed, more advanced than guns — the kinds of early guns the Free Kingdomers had before they switched to silimatic technology.

Horses, though . . . I've never bought that one.

"Okay, look," I said. "Horses are *not* more advanced than cars."

"Sure they are," Patty said.

"Why?"

"Simple. Poop."

I blinked. "Poop?"

"Yup. What do those slobomobiles make? Foul-smelling gas. What do horses make?"

"Poop?"

"Poop," she said. "Fertilizer. You get to go somewhere, *and* you get a useful by-product."

I sat back, feeling a little bit disturbed. Not because of what Patty said — I was used to Free Kingdomer rationalizations. No, I was disturbed because I'd somehow managed to talk about both excrement and flatulence in the course of two chapters.

If I could somehow work in barfing, then I'd have a complete potty humor trifecta.

Riding in the carriage allowed me a good look at the city's people, buildings, and shops. Oddly, I was just surprised by how . . . well, normal everyone seemed. Yes, there were castles. Yes, the people wore tunics and robes instead of slacks and blouses. But the expressions on their faces — the laughter, the frustration, even the boredom — were just like those back home.

Actually, riding down that busy road — with the castle peaks rising like jagged mountains into the sky — felt an awful lot like riding in a taxi through New York City. People are people. Wherever they come from or whatever they look like, they're the same. As the philosopher Garnglegoot the Confused once said: "I'll have a banana and crayon sandwich, please." (Garnglegoot always did have trouble staying on topic.)

"So where do all of these people live?" I asked, then cringed, expecting Bastille to shoot back something like "In their homes, stupid." It took me a second to remember that Bastille wasn't there to make fun of me. That made me sad, though I should have been happy to avoid the mockery.

"Oh, most of them are from Nalhalla City here," Patty said. "Though a fair number of them probably traveled in today via Transporter's Glass."

"Transporter's Glass?"

Aunt Patty nodded her blond-haired head. "It's some very interesting technology, just developed by the Kuanalu Institute over in Halaiki using sands your father discovered a number of years ago. It lets people cross great distances in an instant, using a feasibly economic expenditure of brightsand. I've read some very exciting research on the subject."

I blinked. I believe I've mentioned how unreasonably scholarly the Smedry clan is. A remarkable number of them are professors, researchers, or scientists. We're like an unholy mix of the Brady Bunch and the UCLA honors department.

"You're a professor, aren't you?" I accused.

"Why, yes, dear!" Aunt Patty said.

"Silimatics?"

"That's right; how'd you guess?"

"Just lucky," I said. "Have you ever heard of a theory that says Oculators can power technological types of glass in addition to their Lenses?"

She harrumphed. "Been speaking with your father, I see."

"My father?"

"I'm well aware of that paper he wrote," Aunt Patty continued, "but I don't buy it. Claiming that Oculators were somehow brightsand in human form. Doesn't that seem silly to you? How can sand be human in form?"

"I —"

"I'll admit that there *are* some discrepancies," she continued, ignoring my attempt to interject. "However, your father is jumping to conclusions. This will require *far* more research than he's put into it! Research by people who are more practiced at true silimatics than that scoundrel. Oh, looks like you're getting a zit on your nose, by the way. Too bad that man in the carriage next to us just took a picture of you."

I jumped, glancing to the side where another carriage had pulled up. The man there was holding up squares of glass about a foot on each side, pointing them toward us, then tapping them. I was still new to all this, but I was pretty sure he was doing something very similar to taking pictures with a camera. When he noticed my attention, he lowered his panes of glass, tipped his cap toward me, and his carriage pulled away.

"What was that all about?" I asked.

"Well, hon, you *are* the heir of the Smedry line — not to mention an Oculator raised inside the Hushlands. That kind of thing interests people."

"People *know* about me?" I asked, surprised. I knew I'd been born in Nalhalla, but I'd just assumed that the people in the Free Kingdoms had forgotten.

"Of course they do! You're a celebrity, Alcatraz — the Smedry who disappeared mysteriously as a child! There have been *hundreds* of books written on you. When it came out a few years back that you were being raised in the Hushlands, that only made things more interesting. You think all those people over there are staring because of me?"

I'd never been in Nalhalla before (duh) so I hadn't thought it strange that there were people standing along the streets, watching the road. Now, however, I noticed how many of them were pointing toward our carriage.

"Shattering Glass," I whispered. "I'm *Elvis*."

You Free Kingdomers may not know that name. Elvis was a powerful monarch from Hushlander past, known for his impassioned speeches to inmates, for his odd footwear, and for looking less like himself than the people who dress like him. He vanished mysteriously as the result of a Librarian cover-up.

"I don't know who that is, hon," Aunt Patty said. "But whoever he is, he's probably a lot less well known than you are."

I sat back, stunned. Grandpa Smedry and the others had *tried* to explain how important our family was, but I'd never really understood. We had a castle as large as the king's palace. We controlled incredible wealth. We had magical powers that others envied. There had been volumes and volumes of books written about us.

That was the moment, riding in that carriage, when it all finally hit me. I understood. *I'm famous*, I thought, a smile growing on my face.

This was a very important point in my life. It's where I started to realize just how much power I had. I didn't find fame intimidating. I found it exciting. Instead of hiding from the people with their silimatic cameras, I started waving to them. They began to point even more excitedly, and the attention made me feel good. Warm, like I'd suddenly been bathed in sunlight.

Some say that fame is a fleeting thing. Well, it has clung to me tenaciously, like gum stuck to the sidewalk, blackened from being stepped on a thousand times. I haven't been able to shake it, no matter what.

Some also say fame is shallow. That's easy to say when you haven't spent your childhood being passed from family to family, scorned and discarded because of a curse that made you break whatever you touched.

Fame is like a cheeseburger. It might not be the best or most healthy thing to have, but it will still fill you up. You don't really care how healthy something is when you've been without for so long. Like a cheeseburger, fame fills a need, and it tastes so good going down.

It isn't until years later that you realize what it has done to your heart.

"Here we are!" Aunt Patty said as the carriage slowed. I was surprised. After hearing that my cousin Folsom was in charge of guarding former Librarians, I'd expected to be taken to some sort of police station or secret service hide-out. Instead, we'd come to a shopping district with little stores set into the fronts of the castles. Aunt Patty paid our driver with some glass coins, then climbed down.

"I thought you said he was guarding a Librarian spy," I said, getting out.

"He is, hon."

"And where does one do that?"

Aunt Patty pointed toward a store that looked suspiciously like an ice cream parlor. "Where else?"

CHAPTER 6

Once, when I was very young, I was being driven to the public swimming pool by my foster mother. This was a long time ago, so far distant in my memory I can barely remember it. I must have been three or four years old.

I recall an image: a group of strangely shaped buildings beside the road. I'd seen them before, and I'd always wondered what they were. They looked like small white domes, three or four of them, the size of houses.

As we passed, I turned to my foster mother. "Mom, what are those?"

"That is where the crazy people go," she said.

I hadn't realized there was a mental institution in my town. But it was nice to know where it was. For years after that, when the topic of mental illness came up, I'd explain where the hospital was. I was proud, as a child, to know where they took the crazy people when they went . . . well, crazy.

When I was twelve or so, I remember being driven past that place again with a different foster family. By then, I could read. (I was quite advanced for my age, you know.) I noticed the sign hanging on the domelike buildings.

It didn't say the buildings were a mental institution. It said that they were a church.

Suddenly, I understood. "That's where all the crazy people go" meant something completely different to my foster mother than it had to me. I spent all those years proudly telling people where the asylum was, all the while ignorant of the fact that I'd been completely wrong.

This will all relate.

I stepped into the ice cream shop, trying to be ready for anything. I had seen coolers that turned out to hide banquet rooms. I had seen libraries that hid a dark hideout for cultists. I figured that a place that looked like an ice cream shop was probably something entirely different, like an explosive crayon testing facility. (Ha! That's what you get for writing on the walls, Jimmy!)

If, indeed, the ice cream parlor was fake, it was doing a really good job of that fakery. It looked exactly like something from the fifties, including colorful pastels, stools by the tables, and waitresses in striped red-and-white skirts. Though said waitresses *were* serving banana splits and chocolate shakes to a bunch of people dressed in medieval clothing.

A sign on the wall proudly proclaimed the place to be an AUTHENTIC HUSHLANDER RESTAURANT! When Aunt Patty and I entered, the place grew still. Outside, others were clustering around the windows, looking in at me.

"It's all right, folks," Aunt Patty proclaimed. "He's really not all that interesting. Actually, he kind of smells, so you probably want to keep your distance."

I blushed deeply.

"Notice how I keep them from fawning over you?" she said, patting me on the shoulder. "You can thank me later, hon. I'll go fetch Folsom!" Aunt Patty pushed her way through the busy room. As soon as she was gone, Free Kingdomers began to approach me, ignoring her warning. They were hesitant, though; even the middle-aged men seemed as timid as children.

"Um . . . can I help you?" I asked as I was surrounded.

"You're him, aren't you?" one of them asked. "Alcatraz the Lost."

"Well, I don't feel that lost," I said, growing uncomfortable. To have them so close and so in awe . . . well, I didn't quite know how to react. What was the proper protocol for a long-lost celebrity when first revealing himself to the world?

A young fan, maybe seven years old, solved the problem. He stepped up, holding a square piece of glass five or six inches across. It was clear and flat, as if it had been cut right out of a windowpane. He offered the glass to me with a shaking hand.

Okay, I thought, *that's weird.* I reached out and took the glass. As soon as I touched it, the glass began to glow. The boy pulled it back eagerly, and I could see that my thumb and fingers had left glowing prints. Apparently, this was the Free Kingdomer version of getting an autograph.

The others began to press forward. Some had squares of glass. Others wanted to shake my hand, get their pictures taken with me, or have me use my Talent to break something of theirs as a memento. The bustle might have annoyed someone else, but after a childhood of being alternately mocked (for breaking things) and feared (for breaking things), I was ready for a little bit of adulation.

After all, didn't I deserve it? I'd stopped the Librarians from getting the Sands of Rashid. I'd defeated Blackburn. I'd saved my father from the horrors of the Library of Alexandria.

Grandpa Smedry was right; it was time to relax and enjoy myself. I made thumbprints, posed for pictures, shook hands, and answered questions. By the time Aunt Patty returned, I had launched into a dramatic telling of my first infiltration with Grandpa Smedry. That day in the ice cream parlor was the day I realized that I might make a good writer. I seemed to have a flair for storytelling. I teased the audience with information about what was coming, never quite revealing the ending but hinting at it.

By the way, did you know that later that day, someone was going to try to assassinate King Dartmoor?

"All right, all right," Aunt Patty said, shoving aside some of my fans. "Give the boy some room." She grabbed me by the arm. "Don't worry, hon, I'll rescue you."

"But —!"

"No need to thank me," Aunt Patty said. Then, in a louder voice, she proclaimed, "Everyone, stay back! Alcatraz has been in the Hushlands! You won't want to catch any of his crazy-strange Librarian diseases!"

I saw numerous people's faces pale, and the crowd backed away. Aunt Patty then led me to a table occupied by two people. One, a young man in his twenties with black hair and a hawkish face, looked vaguely familiar. I realized this must be Folsom Smedry; he looked a lot like his brother, Quentin. The young woman seated across from him wore a maroon skirt and white blouse. She had dark skin and her spectacles had a chain.

To be honest, I hadn't expected the Librarian to be so pretty, or so young. Certainly, none of the ones I'd met so far had been pretty. Granted, most of those had been trying to kill me at the time, so perhaps I was a little biased.

Folsom stood up. "Alcatraz!" he said, holding out a hand. "I'm Folsom, your cousin."

"Nice to meet you," I said. "What's your Talent?" (I'd learned by now to ask Smedrys that as soon as I met them. Sitting down to eat with a Smedry without knowing their Talent was a little like accepting a grenade without knowing if the pin had been pulled or not.)

Folsom smiled modestly as we shook hands. "It's not really all that important a Talent. You see, I can dance really poorly."

"Ah," I said. "How impressive."

I tried to sound sincere. I had trouble. It's just so hard to compliment someone for being a bad dancer.

Folsom smiled happily, releasing my hand and gesturing for me to sit. "Great to finally meet you," he said. "Oh, and I'd give that handshake a four out of six."

I sat down. "Excuse me?"

"Four out of six," he said, sitting. "Reasonable firmness with good eye contact, but you held on a little bit long. Anyway, may I present Himalaya Rockies, formerly of the Hushlands?"

I glanced over at the Librarian, then hesitantly held out my hand. I half expected her to pull out a gun and shoot me. (Or at least to chastise me for my overdue books.)

"Pleased to meet you," she said, taking my hand without even trying to stab me. "I hear you grew up in America like I did."

I nodded. She had a Boston accent. I'd only been away from the United States for a couple of weeks, and I had been very eager to escape, but it still felt good to hear someone from my homeland.

"So, er, you're a Librarian?" I asked.

"A *recovering* Librarian," she said quickly.

"Himalaya defected six months ago," Folsom said. "She brought lots of great information for us."

Six months, eh? I thought, eyeing Folsom. He didn't give any indication, but if it had been six months, I found it odd that we were still keeping track of Himalaya. Folsom and the king, I figured, must still worry that she was secretly a spy for the Librarians.

The booths around us filled quickly, and the parlor enjoyed quite a boost in business from my patronage. The owner must have noticed this, for he soon visited our table. "The famous Alcatraz Smedry, in my humble establishment!" he said. The pudgy man wore a pair of bright red-and-white-striped pants. He waved to one of his waitresses, who rushed over with a bowl filled with whipped cream. "Please have a bandana split on the house!"

"Bandana?" I asked, cocking my head.

"They get a few things wrong here," Himalaya whispered, "but it's still the closest you'll get to American food while in Nalhalla."

I nodded thankfully to the owner, who smiled with pleasure. He left a handful of mints on the table, though I don't quite know why, then went back to serving customers. I glanced at the dessert he'd provided. It was, indeed, a large bandana filled with ice cream. I tasted it hesitantly, but it actually was kind of good, in an odd way. I couldn't quite place the flavor.

That probably should have worried me.

"Alcatraz Smedry," Folsom said, as if taking the name for a test drive. "I have to admit, your latest book was a disappointment. One and a half stars out of five."

I had a moment of panic, thinking he referred to the second book of my autobiography. However, I soon realized that was silly, since it not only hadn't been written yet but I didn't even know that I *would* write it. I promptly stopped that line of thinking before I caused a temporal rift and ended up doing something silly, like killing a butterfly or interfering with mankind's first warp jump.

"I have no idea what you're talking about," I said, taking another bite of ice cream.

"Oh, I have it here somewhere," Folsom said, rifling in his shoulder bag.

"I didn't think it was so bad," Himalaya said. "Of course, my tastes *are* tainted by ten years as a Librarian."

"Ten years?" I asked. She didn't look much older than twenty-five to me.

"I started young," she explained, playing idly with the

mints on the table. "I apprenticed to a master Librarian after I'd proven my ability to use the reverse lighthouse system."

"The what?"

"That's when you arrange a group of books alphabetically based on the third letter of the author's mother's maiden name. Anyway, once I got in, the Librarians let me live the high life for a time — buttering me up with advanced reader copies of books and the occasional bagel in the break room. When I was eighteen, they began introducing me into the cult."

She shivered, as if remembering the horrors of those early days. I wasn't buying it, though. As pleasant as she was, I was still suspicious of her motives.

"Ah," Folsom said, pulling something out of his pack. "Here it is." He set a book on the table — one that appeared to have a painting of *me* on the cover. Me riding an enormous vacuum cleaner while wearing a sombrero. I held a flintlock rifle in one hand and what appeared to be a glowing, magical credit card in the other.

Alcatraz Smedry and the Mechanic's Wrench, it read.

"Oh, dear," Aunt Patty said. "Folsom, don't tell me you read those dreadful fantasy novels!"

"They're fun, Mother," he said. "Meaningless, really, but as a diversion I give the genre three out of four marks. This one here was terrible, though. It had all the elements of a great story — a mystical weapon, a boy on a journey, quirky sidekicks. But it ended up ruining itself by trying to say something important, rather than just being amusing."

"That's me!" I said, pointing at the cover.

If Bastille were there, she'd have said something pithy, such as "Glad you can recognize your own face, Smedry. Be careful not to wear a mustache, though. Might confuse yourself."

Unfortunately, Bastille wasn't there. Once again, I found myself annoyed, and once again, I found myself annoyed at myself for being annoyed, which probably annoys you. I know it annoys my editor.

"It's a fictionalized account, of course," Folsom said about the book. "Most scholars know that you didn't do any of these things. However, you're such a part of the cultural unconsciousness that stories about you are quite popular."

The cultural what? I thought, bemused. People were writing books about me! Or, at least, books with me as the hero. That seemed pretty darn cool, even if the facts were sketchy.

"That's the kind of thing they think happens in the Hushlands," Himalaya said, smiling at me, still playing idly with the mints. "Epic battles with the Librarians using strange Hushlander technology. It's all very romanticized and exaggerated."

"Fantasy novels," Aunt Patty said, shaking her head. "Ah, well. Rot your brain if you want. You're old enough that I can't tell you what to do, though I'm glad you kicked that bed-wetting habit before you moved out!"

"Thanks, Mother," Folsom said, blushing. "That's . . . well, that's really nice. We should —" He cut off, glancing at Himalaya. "Um, you're doing it again."

The former Librarian froze, then looked down at the mints in front of her. "Oh, bother!"

"What?" I asked.

"She was classifying them," Folsom said, pointing at the mints. "Organizing them by shape, size, and . . . it appears, color as well."

The mints sat in a neat little row, color coordinated and arranged by size. "It's just so hard to kick the habit," Himalaya said with frustration. "Yesterday, I found myself cataloging the tiles on my bathroom floor, counting the number of each color and the number of chipped ones. I can't seem to stop!"

"You'll beat it eventually," Folsom said.

"I hope so," she said with a sigh.

"Well," Aunt Patty said, standing. "I've got to get back to the court discussion. Folsom should be able to give you the information you want, Alcatraz."

We bid farewell, and Aunt Patty made her way from the room — though not before pointing out to the owner that he *really* ought to do something about his bad haircut.

"What information is it you wanted?" Folsom asked.

I eyed Himalaya, trying to decide just what I wanted to say in front of her.

"Don't worry," Folsom said. "She's completely trustworthy."

If that's the case, then why does she need a guard to watch over her? I didn't buy that Folsom was needed to accustom her to life in the Free Kingdoms — not after six months. Unfortunately, there didn't seem to be any getting around talking with her there, so I decided to explain. I didn't think I'd be revealing anything *too* sensitive.

"My grandfather and I would like a report on Librarian activities here in the city," I said. "I understand you're the one to come to about that sort of thing."

"Well, I *do* have a good time keeping an eye on Librarians," Folsom said with a smile. "What do you want to know?"

I didn't honestly know, as I was still kind of unused to this hero stuff. Whatever the Librarians had been up to lately probably had something to with their current attempt to conquer Mokia, but I didn't know what specifically to look for.

"Anything that seems suspicious," I said, trying to sound suave for my fans, in case any of them were eavesdropping. (Being awesome is hard work.)

"Well, let's see," Folsom said. "This treaty mess started about six months back, when a contingent from the Wardens of the Standard showed up in the city, claiming they wanted to set up an embassy. The king was suspicious, but after years of trying hard to get the Librarians to engage in peace talks, he couldn't really turn them down."

"Six months?" I asked. That would be a little bit after Grandpa Smedry left for the Hushlands to check in on me. It was also about the length of time a frozen burrito would stay in the freezer without turning totally nasty. (I know this because it's very heroic and manly.)

"That's right," Himalaya said. "I was one of the Librarians who came to staff the embassy. That's how I escaped."

I actually hadn't made that connection, but I nodded, as if that were exactly what I'd been thinking, as opposed to comparing my manliness to a frozen food.

"Anyway," Folsom continued, "the Librarians announced they were going to offer us a treaty. Then they started going to parties and socializing with the city's elite."

That sounded like the kind of information my grand-father wanted. I wondered if I should just grab Folsom and take him back.

But, well, Grandfather wouldn't be back to the castle for hours yet. Besides, I was no errand boy. I hadn't simply come to fetch Folsom and then sit around and wait. Alcatraz Smedry, brave vacuum cleaner rider and wearer of the awe-some sombrero, didn't stand for things like that. He was a man of action!

"I want to meet with some of these Librarians," I found myself saying. "Where can we find them?"

Folsom looked concerned. "Well, I guess we could head to the embassy."

"Isn't there somewhere else we could find them? Someplace a little more neutral?"

"There will probably be some at the prince's lunch party," Himalaya said.

"Yeah," Folsom said. "But how will we get into *that*? You have to RSVP months in advance."

I stood up, making a decision. "Let's go. Don't worry about getting us in — I'll handle that."

CHAPTER 7

Okay, **go back** and reread the introductions to chapters two, five, and six. Don't worry, I can wait. I'll go make some popcorn.

Pop. Pop-pop. Pop-pop-pop. Pop. POP!

What, done already? You must not have read very carefully. Go back and do it again.

Munch. Munch-munch. Munch-munch-munch. Munch. Crunch.

Okay, that's better. You should have read about:

1) Fish sticks

2) Several things you can do to fight the Librarians

3) Mental hospitals that are really churches

The connection between these three things should be readily obvious to you:

Socrates.

Socrates was a funny little Greek man best known for forgetting to write things down and for screaming, "Look, I'm a philosopher!" in the middle of a No Philosophy zone. (He was later forced to eat his words. Along with some poison.)

Socrates was the inventor of something very important: the question. That's right, before Socrates, languages had no ability to ask questions. Conversations went like this:

Blurg: "Gee, I wish there were a way I could speak to Grug and see if he's feeling all right."

Grug: "By the tone of your voice, I can tell that you are curious about my health. Since I just dropped this rock on my foot, I would like to request your help."

Blurg: "Alas, though our language has developed the imperative form, we have yet to discover a method of using the interrogative. If only there were a simple way to ease communication between us."

Grug: "I see that a Pteroydeactyl has begun to chew on your head."

Blurg: "Yes, you are quite right. Ouch."

Fortunately, Socrates eventually came along and invented the question, allowing people like Blurg and Grug to speak in a way that wasn't quite so awkward.

All right, I'm lying. Socrates didn't invent the question. But he *did* popularize it through something we call the Socratic method. In addition, he taught people to ask questions about everything. To take nothing for granted.

Ask. Wonder. Think.

And that's the final thing you can do to help fight the evil Librarians. That, and buy lots of my books. (Or did I mention that one already?)

"So, who's this prince that's throwing the party?" I asked as Folsom, Himalaya, and I traveled by carriage.

"The High King's son," Folsom said. "Rikers Dartmoor. Out of seven crowns, I'd give him five and a half. He's likable and friendly, but he doesn't have his father's brilliance."

I'd been trying for a while to figure out why Folsom rated everything like that. So I asked: "Why do you rate everything all the time like that?" (Thanks, Socrates!)

"Hum?" Folsom asked. "Oh, well, I *am* a critic."

"You are?"

He nodded proudly. "Head literary critic for the *Nalhallan Daily*, and a staff writer for plays as well!"

I should have known. Like I said, all of the Smedrys seemed to be involved in one academic field or another.

This was the worst yet. I looked away, suddenly feeling self-conscious.

"Shattering Glass!" Folsom said. "Why do people always get like that when they find out?"

"Get like what?" I asked, trying to act like I wasn't trying to act like anything at all.

"Everyone grows worried when they're around a critic," Folsom complained. "Don't they understand that we can't properly evaluate them if they're not acting *normal*?"

"Evaluate?" I squeaked. "You're evaluating me?"

"Well, sure," Folsom said. "Everybody evaluates. We critics are just trained to talk about it."

That didn't help. In fact, that made me even more uncomfortable. I glanced down at the copy of *Alcatraz Smedry and the Mechanic's Wrench*. Was Folsom judging how much I acted like the hero in the book?

"Oh, don't let that thing annoy you," Himalaya said. She was sitting next to me on the seat, uncomfortably close, considering how little I trusted her. Her voice sounded so friendly. Was that a trick?

"What do you mean?" I asked.

"The book," she said, pointing. "I know it's probably bothering you how trite and ridiculous it is."

I looked down at the cover again. "Oh, I don't know, it's not *that* bad. . . ."

"Alcatraz, you're riding a *vacuum cleaner.*"

"And a noble steed he was. Or, er, well, he appears to be one. . . ." Somewhere deep — hidden far within me, next to the nachos I'd had for dinner a few weeks back — a piece of me acknowledged that she was right. The story did seem rather silly.

"It's a good thing that copy is Folsom's," Himalaya continued. "Otherwise we'd have to listen to that dreadful theme music every time you opened the book. Folsom removes the music plate before he reads the books."

"Why's he do that?" I asked, disappointed. *I have theme music?*

"Ah," Folsom said. "Here we are!"

I looked up as the carriage pulled to a halt outside a very tall, red-colored castle. It had a wide green lawn (the type that was randomly adorned with statues of people who were missing body parts) and numerous carriages parked in front. Our driver brought us right up to the front gates, where several men in white uniforms stood about looking very butler-y.

One stepped up to our carriage. "Invitation?" he asked.

"We don't have one," Folsom said, blushing.

"Ah, well, then," the butler said, pointing. "You can pull around that direction to leave, then —"

"We don't need an invitation," I said, gathering my confidence. "I'm Alcatraz Smedry."

The butler gave me a droll glance. "I'm sure you are. Now, you go that way to leave —"

"No," I said, standing up. "Really, I'm him. Look." I held up the book cover.

"You forgot your sombrero," the butler said flatly.

"But it does look like me."

"I'll admit that you are a good look-alike, but I *hardly* think that a mythical legend has suddenly appeared just so that he can go to a lunch party."

I blinked. It was the first time in my life someone had refused to believe that *I* was *me*.

"Surely you recognize me," Folsom said, stepping up beside me. "Folsom Smedry."

"The critic," the butler said.

"Er, yes," Folsom replied.

"The one who panned His Highness's latest book."

"Just . . . well, trying to offer some constructive advice," Folsom said, blushing again.

"You should be ashamed of trying to use an Alcatraz imposter to insult His Highness at his own party. Now, if you'll just pull along in that direction . . ."

This was getting annoying. So I did the first thing that came to mind. I broke the butler's clothing.

It wasn't that hard. My Talent is very powerful, if a little tough to control. I simply reached out and touched the butler's sleeve, then sent a burst of breaking power into his shirt. Once, this would have simply made it fall off — but I was learning to control my abilities. So, first I made the white uniform turn pink, *then* I made it fall off.

The butler stood in his underwear, pointing into the distance with a naked arm, pink clothing around his feet. "Oh," he finally said. "Welcome, then, Lord Smedry. Let me lead you to the party."

"Thank you," I replied, hopping down from the carriage.

"That was easy," Himalaya said, joining Folsom and me. The butler led the way, still wearing only his underwear, but walking in a dignified manner regardless.

"The breaking Talent," Folsom said, smiling. "I forgot about it! It's extremely rare, and there's only one person alive — mythical legend or not — who has it. Alcatraz, that was a five out of five point five maneuver."

"Thanks," I said. "But what book of the prince's did you give such a bad review to?"

"Er, well," Folsom said. "Did you ever look at the *author* of the book you're carrying?"

I glanced down with surprise. The fantasy novel bore a name on the front that — in the delight of looking at my own name — I'd completely missed. Rikers Dartmoor.

"The prince is a *novelist*?" I asked.

"His father was terribly disappointed to hear about the hobby," Folsom said. "You know what terrible people authors tend to be."

"They're mostly social miscreants," Himalaya agreed.

"Fortunately, the prince has mostly avoided the worst habits of authors," Folsom said. "Probably because writing is only a hobby for him. Anyway, he's fascinated with the Hushlands and with mythological things like motorcycles and eggbeaters."

Great, I thought as we walked through the castle doorway. The corridors inside held framed classic-era movie posters from the Hushlands. Cowboys, *Gone with the Wind*, B movies with slime monsters. I began to understand where the prince got his strange ideas about life in the United States.

We entered a large ballroom. It was filled with people in fancy clothing, holding drinks and chatting. A group of musicians played music by rubbing their fingers on crystal cups.

"Uh-oh," Himalaya said, grabbing Folsom as he started to jerk erratically. Himalaya pulled him out of the room.

"What?" I asked, turning with shock, prepared for an attack.

"It's nothing," she said, stuffing cotton balls into Folsom's ears. I didn't have time to comment on the strange behavior as the mostly naked butler cleared his throat. He pointed at me and proclaimed with a loud voice, "Lord Alcatraz Smedry and guests." Then he turned around and walked away.

I stood awkwardly at the doorway, suddenly aware of my bland clothing: T-shirt and jeans, with a green jacket. The people before me didn't seem to be dressed in any one style — some were wearing medieval gowns or hose, others had what looked to be antiquated vests and suits. All were better dressed than I was.

A figure suddenly pushed to the front of the crowd. The

thirty-something man was wearing lavish robes of blue and silver, and had a short red beard. He also wore a bright red baseball cap on his head. This was undoubtedly Rikers Dartmoor, novelist, prince, fashion mistake.

"You're here!" the prince said, grabbing and shaking my hand. "I can barely contain myself! Alcatraz Smedry, in the flesh! I hear you exploded upon landing in the city!"

"Yes, well," I said. "It wasn't that bad an explosion, all things considered."

"Your life is so exciting!" Rikers said. "Just like I imagined it. And now you're at *my* party! And who is this with you?" His face fell as he recognized Folsom, whose ears were now stuffed with cotton. "Oh, the critic," the prince said. Then, more softly, "Well, I guess we can't help who we're related to, can we?" He winked at me. "Please, come in! Let me introduce you to everyone!"

And he meant *everyone*.

When I first wrote this next section of the book, I tried to be very accurate and detailed. Then I realized that's just plain boring. This is a story about evil Librarians, Teleporting Glass, and sword fights. It's not a book about dumb parties. So, instead, I'm just going to summarize what happened next:

Person one: "Alcatraz, you're so awesome!"

Me: "Yes, I know I am."

The prince: "I always knew he was. Have you read my latest book?"

Person two: "Alcatraz, you are more awesome even than yourself."

Me: "Thank you. I think."

The prince: "He's my buddy, you know. I write books about him."

This went on for the better part of an hour or so. Only, it wasn't boring for me at the time. I enjoyed it immensely. People were paying attention to me, telling me about how wonderful I was. I actually started to believe I *was* the Alcatraz from Rikers's stories. It became a little hard to focus on why I'd come to the party in the first place. Mokia could wait, right? It was important that I get to know people, right?

Eventually, Prince Rikers brought me to the lounge, chatting about how they'd managed to make his books play music. In the lounge, people sat in comfortable chairs, making small talk while they sipped exotic drinks. We passed a large group of partygoers laughing together, and they seemed focused on someone I couldn't see.

Another celebrity, I thought. *I should be gracious to them — I wouldn't want them to get jealous of how much more popular I am than they are.*

We approached the group. Prince Rikers said, "And, of course, you already know this next person."

"I do?" I asked, surprised. The figure in the middle of the crowd of people turned toward me.

It was my father.

I stopped in place. The two of us looked at each other. My father had a large group of people doting on him, and most of them — I noticed — were attractive young women. The types who wore gowns that were missing large chunks of cloth on the back or on the sides.

"Attica!" the prince said. "I must say, your son is proving to be quite a popular addition to the party!"

"Of course he is," my father said, taking a sip of his drink. "He's *my* son, after all."

The way he said it bothered me. It was as if he implied that all of my fame and notoriety were simply because of him. He smiled at me — one of those fake smiles you see on TV — then turned away and said something witty. The women twittered adoringly.

That completely ruined my morning. When the prince

tried to pull me away to meet some more of his friends, I complained of a headache and asked if I could sit down. I soon found myself in a dim corner of the lounge, sitting in a plush chair. The soft, whisperlike sounds of the crystal music floated over the buzz of chattering people. I sipped some fruit juice.

What right did my father have to act so dismissive of me? Hadn't *I* been the one to save his life? I'd grown up inside the Hushlands, oppressed by the Librarians, all because *he* wasn't responsible enough to take care of me.

Of all the people in the room, shouldn't he be the one who was most proud of me?

I should probably say something to lighten the tone here, but I find it hard. The truth was that I didn't feel like laughing, and I don't really think *you* should either. (If you must, you can imagine the butler in his underpants again.)

"Alcatraz?" a voice asked. "Can we join you?"

I looked up to find Folsom and Himalaya being held back by the servant left to guard me. I waved for him to let them pass, and they took seats near me.

"Nice party," Folsom said in an overly loud voice. "I give it four out of five wineglasses, though the finger food only rates a one and a half."

I made no comment.

"Did you find what you were looking for?" Folsom asked in a loud voice. His ears were still stuffed with cotton for some reason.

Had I found what I was looking for? What had I been looking for? *Librarians*, I thought. *That's right.* "I didn't see any Librarians around."

"What do you mean?" Himalaya said. "They're all over the place."

They were? "Er . . . I mean, I didn't see them doing anything nefarious."

"They're up to something," Himalaya said. "I bet you anything. There are a *lot* of them here. Look, I made a list."

I looked over with surprise and embarrassment as she handed me a sheet of paper.

"They're listed by their Librarian sect," she said, somewhat apologetically. "Then by age. Then, uh, by height." She glanced at Folsom. "Then by blood type. Sorry. Couldn't help it."

"What?" he asked, having trouble hearing.

I scanned the list. There were some forty people on it. I really *had* been distracted. I didn't recognize any of the names, but —

I cut off as I read a name near the bottom of the list. *Fletcher.*

"Who is this?" I demanded, pointing at the name.

"Hum?" Himalaya asked. "Oh. I only saw her once. I don't know which of the orders she belongs to."

"Show me," I said, standing.

Himalaya and Folsom rose and led me through the ballroom.

"Hey, Alcatraz!" a voice called as we walked.

I turned to see a richly dressed group of young men waving at me. One of those at their lead, a man named Rodrayo, was a minor nobleman the prince had introduced me to. Everyone seemed so eager to be my friend; it was difficult not to join them. However, the name on that list — Fletcher — was too intimidating. I waved apologetically to Rodrayo, then continued with Himalaya.

A few moments later, she laid a hand on my shoulder. "There," she said, pointing at a figure who was making her way out the front doors. The woman had dyed her hair dark brown since I'd last seen her, and she wore a Free Kingdomer gown instead of her typical business suit.

But it was her: my mother. Ms. Fletcher was an alias. I felt a sudden sense of shame for getting so wrapped up in the party. If my mother was in the city, it meant something. She was too businesslike for simple socializing; she was always plotting.

And she had my father's Translator's Lenses.

"Come on," I said to Folsom and Himalaya. "We're following her."

CHAPTER 8

Once there was a boy named Alcatraz. He did some stuff that was kind of interesting. Then one day, he betrayed those who depended on him, doomed the world, and murdered someone who loved him.

The end.

Some people have asked me why I need multiple volumes to explain my story. After all, the core of my argument is very simple. I just told it to you in one paragraph.

Why not leave it at that?

Two words: Summarizing sucks.

Summarizing is when you take a story that is complicated and interesting, then stick it in a microwave until it shrivels up into a tiny piece of black crunchy tarlike stuff. A wise man once said, "Any story, no matter how good, will sound really, really dumb when you shorten it to a few sentences."

For example, take this story: "Once there was a furry-footed British guy who has to go throw his uncle's ring into a hole in the ground." Sounds dumb, doesn't it?

I don't intend to do that. I intend to make you experience each and every painful moment of my life. I intend to prove how dreadful I am by talking about how awesome I am. I intend to make you read through a whole series before explaining the scene in which I started the first book.

You remember that one, right? The one where I lay tied to an altar made from encyclopedias, about to get sacrificed by the Librarians? That's when my betrayal happened. You may be wondering when I'm finally going to get to that most important point in my life.

Book five. So there.

"So who is this person we're following?" Folsom asked, pulling the cotton from his ears as we left the prince's castle.

"My mother," I said curtly, glancing about. A carriage was leaving, and I caught a glance of my mother's face in it. "There. Let's go."

"Wait," Folsom said. "That's *Shasta Smedry*?"

I nodded.

He whistled. "This could get dangerous."

"There's more," Himalaya said, catching up to us. "If what I heard in there is true, then *She Who Cannot Be Named* is going to be arriving in the city soon."

"Wait, who?" I asked.

"I just told you," Himalaya said. "She Who Cannot Be Named. The Librarians aren't satisfied with how the treaty negotiations are proceeding, so they decided to bring in a heavy hitter."

"That's bad," Folsom said.

"She Who Cannot Be Named?" I asked. "Why can't we say her name? Because it might draw the attention of evil powers? Because we're afraid of her? Because her name has become a curse upon the world?"

"Don't be silly," Himalaya said. "We don't say her name because nobody can pronounce it."

"Kangech . . ." Folsom tried. "Kangenchenug . . . Kagenchachsa . . ."

"She Who Cannot Be Named," Himalaya finished. "It's easier."

"Either way," Folsom said, "we should report back to Lord Smedry — this is going to get very dangerous, very quickly."

109

I snorted. "It's no more dangerous than when I testified against the Acrophobic English Teachers of Poughkeepsie!"

"Uh, you didn't actually do that, Alcatraz," he pointed out. "That was in one of the books Rikers wrote."

I froze. That's right. I'd been talking about it with the prince, but that didn't change the fact that it hadn't ever actually happened.

It *also* didn't change the fact that Shasta's carriage was quickly disappearing. "Look," I said, pointing. "My grandfather put you in charge of watching the Librarians in the city. Now you're going to let one of the most infamous ones get away without following?"

"Hum," he said. "Good point."

We rushed down the steps and toward the carriages. I picked a likely one, then hopped up into it. "I'm commandeering this vehicle!" I said.

"Very well, Lord Smedry," said the driver.

I hadn't expected it to be that easy. You should remember that we Smedrys are legal officers of the government in Nalhalla. We're able to commandeer pretty much anything we want. (Only doughnuts are outside our reach, as per the Doughnut Exemption act of the eighth century. Fortunately, doughnuts don't exist in the Free Kingdoms, so the law doesn't get used much.)

Folsom and Himalaya climbed into the carriage after me, and I pointed at Shasta's disappearing vehicle. "Follow that carriage!" I said in a dramatic voice.

And so, the driver did. Now, I don't know if you've ever been in a city carriage before, but they travel at, like, two miles an hour — particularly during afternoon traffic. After my rather dramatic and heroic (if I do say so myself) proclamation, things took a decidedly *slow* turn as our driver guided the horses out onto the street, then clopped along behind Shasta's vehicle. I felt more like I was out on a casual evening drive than part of a high-speed chase.

I sat down. "Not very exciting, is it?"

"I'll admit, I was expecting more," Folsom said.

At that moment, we passed a street performer playing a lute on the side of the road. Himalaya reached for Folsom, but it was too late. My cousin stood up in a quick motion, then jumped up onto the back of the carriage and began doing expert kung fu moves.

"Gak!" I said, diving for the floor as a karate chop narrowly missed my head. "Folsom, what are you doing?"

"It's his Talent," Himalaya said, scrambling down beside me. "He's a bad dancer! The moment he hears music, he gets like this. It —"

We passed the street performer and Folsom froze mid-swing, his foot mere inches from my face. "Oh," he said, "terribly sorry about that, Alcatraz. My Talent can be a bit difficult at times."

"A bit difficult" is an understatement. Folsom once wandered into a ballroom dance competition. He not only managed to trip every single person in the room but he also ended up stuffing one of the judges in a tuba. If you're wondering, yes, that's why Himalaya had filled Folsom's ears with cotton before letting him enter the party room. It's also why Folsom had removed the theme music glass from his copy of *Alcatraz Smedry and the Mechanic's Wrench.*

"Alcatraz!" Himalaya said, pointing as we seated ourselves again.

I spun, realizing that my mother's carriage had stopped at an intersection, and our carriage was pulling up right beside hers. "Gak!" I said. "Driver, what are you doing?"

The driver turned, confused. "Following that carriage, like you said."

"Well, don't let them *know* that we're following them!" I said. "Haven't you ever seen any superspy movies?"

"What's a movie?" the driver asked, followed by, "And . . . what's a superspy?"

I didn't have time to explain. I waved for Himalaya and Folsom to duck. However, there just wasn't enough room — one of us would have to sit up. Would my mother recognize Folsom, a famous Smedry? What about Himalaya, a rebel Librarian? We were all conspicuous.

"Can't you two do something to hide us?" Himalaya hissed. "You know, magic powers and all that."

"I could beat up her horse, if we had music," Folsom said thoughtfully.

Himalaya glanced at me, worried, and it wasn't until that moment that I remembered that I was an Oculator.

Oculator. Lens-wielder. I had magic glasses, including the ones my grandfather had given me earlier. I cursed, pulling out the purple ones he'd called Disguiser's Lenses. He'd told me to think of something, then look at someone, and I would appear to be that thing. I slid the Lenses on and focused.

Himalaya yelped. "You look like an old man!"

"Lord Smedry?" Folsom asked, confused.

That wouldn't do. Shasta would recognize Grandpa Smedry for sure. I threw myself up into the seat and thought of someone else. My sixth-grade teacher, Mr. Mann. I remembered, at the last minute, to picture him wearing a tunic like he was from the Free Kingdoms. Then I looked over at my mother, sitting in the next carriage.

She glanced at me. My heart thumped in my chest. (Hearts tend to do that. Unless you're a zombie. More on those later.)

My mother's eyes passed over me without showing any signs of recognition. I breathed a sigh of relief as the carriages started again.

Using the Disguiser's Lenses was more difficult than any others I'd used before. I got a jolt if my shape changed forms, and that happened whenever I let my mind wander. I had to remain focused to maintain the illusion.

As we continued, I felt embarrassed at taking so long to remember the Disguiser's Lenses. Bastille often chastised me for forgetting that I was an Oculator, and she was right. I still wasn't that used to my powers, as you will see later.

(You'll notice that I often mention ideas I'm going to explain later in the book. Sometimes I do this because it makes nice foreshadowing. Other times, I'm just trying to annoy you. I'll let you decide which is which.)

"Do either of you recognize where we are?" I asked as the carriage "chase" continued.

"We're approaching the king's palace, I think," Folsom said. "Look, you can see the tips of the towers."

I followed his gesture and saw the white peaks of the palace. On the other side of the street, we passed an enormous rectangular building that read in big letters ROYAL ARCHIVES (NOT A LIBRARY!) on the front. We turned, then rolled past a line of castles on the back side of the street. My mother's carriage turned as if to round the block again. Something seemed wrong.

"Driver, catch up to the carriage up there," I said.

"Indecisive today, aren't we?" the driver asked with a sigh. At the next intersection, we rolled up beside the carriage, and I looked over at my mother.

Only, she wasn't there. The carriage held someone who *looked* a little like her, but wasn't the same woman. "Shattering Glass!" I cursed.

"What?" Folsom asked, peeking up over the lip of the carriage.

"She gave us the slip," I said.

"Are you sure that's not her?" Folsom asked.

"Um, yeah. Trust me." I might not have known she was my mother at the time, but "Ms. Fletcher" had watched over me for most of my childhood.

"Maybe she's using Lenses, like you," Himalaya said.

"She's not an Oculator," I replied. "I don't know if she knew she was being followed, but she somehow got out of that carriage when we weren't looking."

The other two got up off the floor, sitting again. I eyed Himalaya. Had she somehow tipped off my mother that we were following?

"Shasta Smedry," Himalaya said. "Is she a relative of yours, then?"

"Alcatraz's mother," Folsom said, nodding.

"Really?" Himalaya said. "Your mother is a recovering Librarian?"

"Not so much on the 'recovering' part," I said. The carriage bearing the look-alike stopped and let her off at a restaurant. I ordered our driver to wait so we could watch, but I knew we wouldn't learn anything new.

"She and his father broke up soon after he was born," Folsom said. "Shasta went back to the Librarians."

"Which order is she part of?"

I shook my head. "I don't know. She . . . doesn't quite fit with the others. She's something different." My grandfather had once said that her motivations were confusing, even to other Librarians.

She had the Lenses of Rashid; if she found an Oculator to help her, she could read the Forgotten Language. That made her very, very dangerous. Why had she been at that party? Had she spoken with my father? Had she been trying to do something to the prince?

"Let's get back to the castle," I said. Perhaps Grandpa Smedry would be able to help.

CHAPTER 9

Chapter breaks are very useful. They let you skip a lot of boring parts of stories. For instance, after tailing — then losing — my mother, we had a pleasant drive back to Keep Smedry. The most exciting thing that happened was when we stopped so that Folsom could use the restroom.

Characters in books, you may have noticed, rarely have to go potty. There are several reasons for this. Many books — unlike this one — simply aren't real, and everyone knows fictional characters can "hold it" as long as they need to. They just wait until the end of the book before using the restroom.

In books like this one, which *are* real, we have more problems. After all, we're not fictional characters, so we have to wait until chapter breaks, when nobody is looking. It can get hard for longer chapters, but we're quite self-sacrificing. (I really feel sorry for the people in Terry Pratchett's novels, though.)

Our carriage pulled up to the dark, stone Keep Smedry, and I was surprised to see a small crowd gathered in front.

"Not this again," Himalaya said with a sigh as some of the people began to wave pieces of glass in my direction, taking images of me in the strange Free Kingdoms way.

"Sorry," Folsom said with a grimace. "We can send them away, if you want."

"Why would we do that?" I asked. After the disappointment of losing Shasta, it felt good to see people eager to praise me again.

Folsom and Himalaya exchanged a look. "We'll be inside, then," Folsom said, helping Himalaya down. I jumped out, then went to meet with my adoring fans.

The first ones to rush up to me carried pads of paper and quills. They all talked over one another, so I tried to quiet them down by raising my hands. That didn't work; they all just kept talking, trying to get my attention.

So I broke the sound barrier.

I'd never done it before, but my Talent can do some really wacky things. I was standing there, frustrated, hands in the air, wishing I could get them to be quiet. Then my

Talent engaged, and there were twin *CRACK* sounds in the air, like a pair of whips snapping.

The people fell silent. I started, surprised by the tiny sonic booms I'd made.

"Er, yes," I said. "What do you want? And before you start arguing, let's start with you on the end."

"Interview," the man said. He wore a hat like Robin Hood. "I represent the Eastern Criers Guild. We want to do a piece on you."

"Oh," I said. That sounded cool. "Yeah, we can do that. But not right now. Maybe later tonight?"

"Before or after the vote?" the man asked.

Vote? I thought. *Oh, right. The vote about the treaty with the Librarians.* "Uh, after the vote."

The others began to talk, so I raised my hands threateningly and quieted them down. All were reporters, wanting interviews. I made appointments with each one, and they went on their way.

The next group of people approached. These didn't appear to be reporters of any sort, which was good. Reporters, it might be noted, are a lot like little brothers. They're talkative, annoying, and they tend to come in groups. Plus, if you yell at them, they get even in very unsettling ways.

"Lord Smedry," a stout man said. "I was wondering . . . My daughter is getting married this upcoming weekend. Would you perform the ceremony?"

"Uh, sure," I said. I'd been warned about this, but it was still something of a surprise.

He beamed, then told me where the wedding was. The next woman in line wanted me to represent her son in a trial and speak on his behalf. I wasn't sure what to do about that one, so I said I'd get back to her. The next man wanted me to seek out — then punish — a miscreant who had stolen some galfalgos from his garden. I made a mental note to ask someone what the heck galfalgos were, and told him I'd look into it.

There were some two dozen people with questions or requests like those. The more that was asked of me, the more uncomfortable I grew. What did I really know about any of this stuff? I finally cleared through that group, making vague promises to most of them.

There was one more group of people waiting for me. They were well-dressed younger men and women, in their late teens or early twenties. I recognized them from the party.

"Rodrayo?" I asked, to the guy at their lead.

"Hey," he said.

"And . . . what is it you want of me?" I asked.

A couple of them shrugged.

"Just thought being around you would be fun," Rodrayo said. "Mind if we party with you a little bit?"

"Oh," I said. "Well, sure, I guess."

I led the group through some hallways in Keep Smedry, getting lost, and trying to act like I knew where everything was. The hallways of Keep Smedry were appropriately medieval, though the castle was far more warm and homey than one might have expected. There were hundreds of rooms — the building was of mansion-sized proportions — and I really didn't know where I was going.

Eventually, I found some servants and had them take us to a denlike room, which had couches and a hearth. I wasn't certain what "partying with me" meant to Rodrayo and the others. Fortunately, they took the lead, sending the servants to get some food, then lounging around on the couches and chairs, chatting. I wasn't sure why they needed me there, or even who most of them were, but they'd read my books and thought my adventures were very impressive. That made them model citizens in my opinion.

I had just finished telling them about my fight with the paper monsters when I realized that I'd never checked in with Grandpa Smedry. It had been about five hours since we'd split up, and I was tempted to just let it slide until he came looking for me. But we needed more hooberstackers, and the servants had vanished, so I decided to leave my new friends and go looking for the servants to ask for a resupply. Maybe they'd know where my grandfather was.

However, finding servants proved more difficult than I'd assumed. I felt uncharacteristically fatigued as I wandered the hallways, even though I hadn't really done that much during the last couple of hours. Just sit around and be adored.

Eventually, I spotted a crack of light down one brick-walled corridor. It turned out to be coming from a half-open door, so I peeked inside. There, I found my father sitting at a desk, scribbling on a piece of parchment. An ancient-looking lamp gave off a flickering light, only faintly illuminating the room. I could see rich-looking furniture and sparkling bits of glass — Lenses and other Oculatory wonders, which seemed to have a glow about them because of my Oculator's Lenses. On his desk was a half-empty wineglass, and he still wore the antiquated suit he'd had on at the party, though he'd undone the ruffled tie. His shoulder-length hair was wavy and disheveled. He looked a lot like a Hushlands rock star after an evening performance.

As a child, I'd often dreamed about what my father would be like. The only facts I'd had to go on were that he'd named me after a prison and that he'd abandoned me. One would think that I would have imagined a terrible person.

And yet, I'd secretly *wished* for there to be more. A good reason why he'd given me up. Something impressive and mysterious. I had wondered if, perhaps, he'd been involved in some dangerous line of work, and had sent me away to protect me.

Grandpa Smedry's arrival, and the discovery that my father was both alive and working to save the Free Kingdoms, fulfilled a lot of these secret wishes. Finally, I gained a picture of who my father might be. A dashing, heroic figure who hadn't *wanted* to get rid of me, but had been betrayed by his wife, then forced to give me up for the greater good.

That father in my dreams would have been excited to reunite with his son. I'd been hoping for enthusiasm, not indifference. I'd imagined someone a little more like Indiana Jones, and a little less like Mick Jagger.

"Mother was there," I said, stepping into the doorway more fully.

My father didn't look up from his document. "Where?" he asked, not even jumping or looking surprised at the intrusion.

"At the party this afternoon. Did you see her?"

"Can't say that I did," my father said.

"I was surprised to see you there."

My father didn't respond; he just scribbled something on his parchment. I couldn't figure him out — at the party, he had seemed completely involved in being a superstar. Now, at his desk, he was absorbed in his work.

"What are you working on?" I asked.

He sighed, finally looking up at me. "I understand that children sometimes need distractions. Is there something I can have the servants bring you? Entertainment? Just speak it, and I shall see it done."

"That's all right," I said. "Thanks."

He nodded and turned back to his work. The room fell still; the only sound was that of his quill scratching against parchment.

I left and didn't feel like searching out servants or my grandfather anymore. I just felt sick. Like I'd eaten three whole bags of Halloween candy, then been punched in the stomach. I wandered, vaguely making my way in the direction of where I'd left my new friends. When I arrived back at the den where I'd left them, however, I was surprised to see them being entertained by an unlikely figure.

"Grandpa?" I asked, looking in.

"Ah, Alcatraz, my boy," Grandpa Smedry said, perched atop a tall-legged chair. "Excellent to see you! I was just explaining to these fine young fellows that you'd be back very soon, and that they shouldn't worry about you."

They didn't seem all that worried, though they *had* found some more snacks somewhere — popcorn and hooberstackers. I stood at the doorway. For some reason, the idea of talking to my groupies in front of Grandpa Smedry made me feel even more sick.

"Not looking too well, my boy," Grandpa Smedry said, rising. "Maybe we should get you something for that."

"I . . . I think that would be nice," I said.

"We'll be back in a snap!" Grandpa Smedry said to the others, hopping off his chair. I followed him down the hallway until he stopped at a darkened stone intersection, turning to me. "I've got the perfect solution, lad! Just the thing to make you feel better in a jiffy!"

"Great," I said. "What is it?"

He smacked me across the face.

I blinked in surprise. It hadn't really hurt, but it *had* been unexpected. "What was that?" I asked.

"I smacked you," said Grandpa Smedry. Then, in a slightly lower tone, he added, "It's an old family remedy."

"For what?"

"Being a nigglenut," said Grandpa Smedry. He sighed, sitting down on the hallway carpeting. "Sit down, lad."

Still a little stunned, I did so.

"I just got done speaking with Folsom and his lovely friend Himalaya," Grandpa Smedry said, pleasantly smiling, as if he hadn't just smacked me in the face. "It seems that they think you are reckless!"

"That's a problem?"

"Velcroed Verns, of course not! I was quite proud to hear that. Recklessness and boldness, great Smedry traits. Thing is, they said some other things about you — things they'd only admit after I pushed them on it."

"What things?"

"That you're self-centered. That you think you're better than regular people, and that all you talk about is yourself. Now, this didn't sound like the Alcatraz I knew. Not at all. So I came back here to investigate — and what did I find? A pile of Attica's sycophants lounging about my castle, just like the old days."

"My *father's* sycophants?" I asked, glancing at the room a little down the hallway. "But they're fans of mine! Not my father's."

"Is that so?"

"Yeah, they've read my books. They talk about them all the time."

"Alcatraz, lad," Grandpa Smedry said. "Have *you* read those books?"

"Well, no."

"Then how the blazes do you know what's in them?"

"Well, I . . ." This was frustrating. Didn't I deserve to finally have someone looking up to me, respecting me? Praising me?

"This is my fault," Grandpa Smedry said with a sigh. "Should have prepared you better for the kinds of people you'd find here. But, well, I thought you'd use the Truthfinder's Lens."

The Truthfinder's Lens. I'd almost forgotten about it —
it could tell me when people were lying. I pulled it free from
my pocket, then glanced at Grandpa Smedry. He nodded
back down the hallway, so hesitantly I stood up and took
off my Oculator's Lenses, walking down the hallway to
the room.

I looked in, holding the Truthfinder's Lens in front of
my eye.

"Alcatraz!" Rodrayo said. "We've missed you!" As he
spoke, he seemed to spit mouthfuls of black beetles from
his mouth. They squirmed and writhed, and I jumped
backward, removing the Lens. The beetles vanished when I
did so. I hesitantly replaced the Lens.

"Alcatraz?" Rodrayo asked. "What's wrong? Come in, we
want to hear more about your adventures."

More beetles. I could only assume that meant he was
lying.

"Hey," said Jasson, "yeah. Those stories are fun!"

Lying.

"There's the greatest man in the city!" another said,
pointing at me.

Lying.

I stumbled away from the room, then fled back down

the hallway. Grandpa Smedry waited for me, still sitting on the floor. "So," I said, sitting down next to him. "It's all lies. Nobody really looks up to me."

"Lad, lad," Grandpa Smedry said, laying a hand on my shoulder. "They don't *know* you. They only know the stories and the legends! Even that lot in there, useless though they tend to be, have their good points. But everyone is going to assume that because they've heard so much about you, they *know* you."

They were wise words. Prophetic, in a way. Ever since I left the Hushlands, I've felt like every person who looked at me saw someone different, and I wasn't any of them. My reputation only grew more daunting after the events at the Library of Congress and the Spire of the World.

"It's not easy to be famous," Grandpa Smedry said. "We all deal with it differently. Your father gluts himself on his fame, then flees from it. I tried for years to teach him to keep his ego in check, but I fear I have failed."

"I thought . . ." I said, looking down. "I thought if he heard people talking about how wonderful I was, he might actually *look* at me once in a while."

Grandpa Smedry fell silent. "Ah, lad," he finally said. "Your father is . . . well, he is what he is. We just have to do our best to love him. But I worry that the fame will do to *you* what it's done to him. That's why I was so excited that you found that Truthfinder's Lens."

"I thought it was for me to use on the Librarians."

"Ha!" Grandpa Smedry said. "Well, it could be of *some* use against them — but a clever Librarian agent will know not to say any direct lies, lest they get caught in them."

"Oh," I said, putting the Truthfinder's Lens away.

"Anyway, you look better, lad! Did the old family remedy work? We can try again if you want. . . ."

"No, I feel much better," I said, holding up my hands. "Thanks, I guess. Though it *was* nice to feel like I had friends."

"You do have friends! Even if you are kind of ignoring them at the moment."

"Ignoring them?" I said. "I haven't been ignoring anyone."

"Oh? And where's Bastille?"

"She ran off on me," I said. "To be with the other knights."

Grandpa Smedry snorted. "To go on trial, you mean."

"An unfair trial," I spat. "She didn't break her sword — it was *my* fault."

"Hum, yes," Grandpa Smedry said. "If only there were someone willing to speak on her behalf."

"Wait," I said. "I can *do* that?"

"What did I tell you about being a Smedry, lad?"

"That we could marry people," I said, "and arrest people, and . . ." And that we could demand a right to testify in legal cases.

I stood up, shocked. "I've been an idiot!"

"I prefer the term 'nigglenut,'" Grandpa Smedry said. "Though that's probably because I just made it up and feel a certain paternal sense toward it." He smiled, winking.

"Is there still time?" I asked. "Before her trial, I mean?"

"It's been going on all afternoon," Grandpa Smedry said, pulling out an hourglass. "And they're probably almost ready to render judgment. Getting there in time will be tricky. Limping Lowrys, if *only* we could teleport there via use of a magical glass box sitting in the basement of this very castle!"

He paused. "Oh, wait, we can!" He leaped to his feet. "Let's go! We're late!"

CHAPTER 10

There's a dreadful form of torture in the Hushlands, devised by the Librarians. Though this is supposed to be a book for all ages, I feel that it's time to confront this disturbing and cruel practice. Somebody has to be brave enough to shine a light on it.

That's right. It's time to talk about after-school specials.

After-school specials are a type of television programming that the Librarians put on right when children get home from school. The specials are usually about some kid who is struggling with a nonsensical problem like bullying, peer pressure, or gerbil snorting. We see the kid's life, his struggles, his problems — and then the show provides a nice, simple solution to tie everything up by the end.

The point of these programs, of course, is to be so blatantly awful and painful to watch that the children wish they were back in school. That way, when they have to get up the next morning and do long division, they'll think: *Well, at least I'm not at home watching that terrible after-school special.*

I include this explanation here for all of you in the Free Kingdoms so that you'll understand what I'm about to say. It's very important for you to understand that I don't want this book to sound like an after-school special.

I let my fame go to my head. The point of this book isn't to show how that's bad, it's to show the truth about me as a person. To show what I'm capable of. That first day in Nalhalla, I think, says a lot about who I am.

I don't even *like* hooberstackers.

Deep within the innards of Keep Smedry, we approached a room with six guards standing out front. They saluted Grandpa Smedry; he responded by wiggling his fingers at them. (He's like that sometimes.)

Inside, we discovered a group of people in black robes who were polishing a large metal box.

"That's quite the box," I said.

"Isn't it, though?" Grandpa Smedry said, smiling.

"Shouldn't we be summoning a dragon or something to take us to Crystallia?"

"This will be faster," Grandpa Smedry said, waving

over one of the people in robes. (Black robes are the Free Kingdoms' equivalent of a white lab coat. Black makes way more sense — this way, when the scientists blow themselves up, at least the robes have a chance of being salvageable.)

"Lord Smedry," the woman said. "We've applied for a Swap Time with Crystallia. Everything will be ready for you in about five minutes."

"Excellent, excellent!" Grandpa Smedry said. Then his face fell.

"What?" I asked, alarmed.

"Well, it's just that . . . we're *early*. I'm not sure what to think about that. You must be having a bad influence on me, my boy!"

"Sorry," I said. It was hard to contain my anxiety. Why hadn't I thought of going to help Bastille? Would I arrive in time to make a difference? If a train left Nalhalla traveling at 3.14 miles an hour and a train left Bermuda at 45 MHz, what time does the soup have pancakes?

"Grandfather," I said as we waited. "I saw my mother today."

"Folsom mentioned that. You showed great initiative in following her."

"She's *got* to be up to something."

"Of course she is, lad. Problem is, what?"

"You think it might be related to the treaty?"

Grandpa Smedry shook his head. "Maybe. Shasta's a tricky one. I don't see her working with the Wardens of the Standard on one of their projects unless it were helping her own goals. Whatever those are."

That seemed to trouble him. I turned back to the robed men and women. They were focused on large chunks of glass that were affixed to the corners of the metal box.

"What is that thing?" I asked.

"Hum? Oh. Transporter's Glass, lad! Or, well, that's Transporter's Glass at the corners of the box. When the right time arrives — the one we've scheduled with the engineers at a similar box up in Crystallia — both groups will shine brightsand on those bits of glass. Then the box will be swapped with the one over in Crystallia."

"Swapped?" I said. "You mean we'll get teleported there?"

"Indeed! Fascinating technology. Your father helped develop it, you know."

"He did?"

"Well, he was the first to discover what the sand did," Grandpa Smedry said. "We'd known that the sand had Oculatory distortions; we didn't know what it *did*. Your father spent a number of years researching it and discovered that this new sand could teleport things. But it only worked if *two* sets of Transporter's Glass were exposed to brightsand at the same time, and if they were transporting two items that were exactly the same size."

Brightsand. It was the fuel of silimatic technology. When you expose other sands to brightsand's glowing light, they do interesting things. Some, for instance, start to float. Others grow very heavy.

I could see enormous canisters in the corners of the room, likely filled with brightsand. The sides of the containers could be pulled back, letting the light shine on the Transporter's Glass.

"So," I said. "You had to send ahead to Crystallia and tell them what time we were coming so that they could activate *their* Transporter's Glass at the same time."

"Precisely!"

"What if someone else activated their brightsand at exactly the same time that we do? Could we get teleported there by accident?"

"I suppose," Grandpa Smedry said. "But they'd have to be sending a box *exactly* the same size as this one. Don't worry, lad. It would be virtually impossible for that kind of error to happen!"

Virtually impossible. The moment you read that, you probably assumed that the error would — of course — happen by the end of this book. You assumed this because you've read far too many novels. You make it very difficult for us writers to spring proper surprises on you because —

LOOK OVER THERE!

See, didn't work, did it?

"All right," one of the black-robed people said. "Step into the box and we'll begin!"

Still a little worried about a disaster that was "virtually" impossible, I followed Grandpa Smedry into the box. It felt a little like stepping into a large elevator. The doors shut, then immediately opened again.

"Is something wrong?" I asked.

"Wrong?" Grandpa Smedry said. "Why, if something had gone wrong, we'd have been shredded to little pieces and turned into piles of sludge!"

"*What?*"

"Oh, did I forget to mention that part?" Grandpa Smedry said. "Like I said, virtually impossible. Come on, my boy, we have to keep moving! We're late!"

He scuttled out of the box, and I followed more cautiously. We had, indeed, been teleported somewhere else. It had been so quick I hadn't even felt the change.

This new room we entered was made completely of glass. In fact, the entire *building* around me seemed to be made of glass. I remembered the enormous glass mushroom I'd seen when flying into the city, with the crystalline castle built atop of it. It was a safe bet I was in Crystallia. Of course, there was *also* a pair of knights holding massive swords made entirely from crystal standing at the doorway. They were kind of a clue too.

The knights nodded to Grandpa Smedry, and he bustled out of the room, and I followed hastily. "We're really there?" I asked. "Atop the mushroom?"

"Yes indeed," Grandpa Smedry said. "It's a rare privilege to be allowed into these halls. Crystallia is forbidden to outsiders."

"Really?"

Grandpa Smedry nodded. "Like Smedrious, Crystallia used to be a sovereign kingdom. During the early days of

Nalhalla, Crystallia's queen married their king and swore her knights as protectors of their noble line. It's actually a rather romantic and dramatic story — one I would eagerly tell you, except for the fact that I recently forgot it based on its being far too long and having not enough decapitations."

"A just reason for forgetting any story."

"I know," Grandpa Smedry said. "Anyway, the treaty that merged Nalhalla and Crystallia stipulated that the land atop the mushroom become home to the knights, and is off-limits to common citizens. The order of knights also retained the right to discipline and train its members, once recruited, without interference from the outside."

"But aren't we here to interfere?"

"Of course we are!" Grandpa Smedry said, raising a hand. "That's the Smedry way! We interfere with all kinds of stuff! But we're also Nalhallan nobility, which the knights are sworn to protect and — most important — not kill for trespassing."

"That's not a very comforting rationale for why we might be safe here."

"Don't worry," Grandpa Smedry said happily. "I've tested this. Just enjoy the view!"

It was tough. Not that the view wasn't spectacular — we were walking down a hallway constructed entirely from glass blocks. It was late afternoon outside, and the translucent walls refracted the light of the sun, making the floor sparkle. I could see shadows of people moving through distant hallways, distorting the light further. It was as if the castle were alive, and I could see the pulsing of its organs within the walls around me.

It was quite breathtaking. However, I was still dealing with the fact that I'd betrayed Bastille, that I'd just risked being turned into a pile of goo, and that the only thing keeping me from being cut apart by a bunch of territorial knights was my last name.

Beyond that, there was the sound. It was a quiet ringing, like a crystal vibrating in the distance. It was soft, but it was also one of those things that was very hard to un-notice once you spotted it.

Grandpa Smedry obviously knew his way around Crystallia, and soon we arrived at a chamber being guarded by two knights. The crystal doors were closed, but I could vaguely make out the shapes of people on the other side.

Grandpa Smedry walked over to open the door, but one

of the knights raised his hand. "You are too late, Lord Smedry," the man said. "The judgment has begun."

"What?" Grandpa Smedry declared. "I was told it wouldn't happen for an hour yet!"

"It is happening now," the knight said. As much as I like the knights, they can be . . . well, blunt. And stubborn. And really bad at taking jokes. (Which is why I feel I need to mention page 40 again, just to annoy them.)

"Surely you can let us in," Grandpa Smedry said. "We're important witnesses in the case!"

"Sorry," the knight said.

"We are also close personal friends of the knight involved."

"Sorry."

"We also have very good teeth," Grandpa Smedry said, then smiled.

This seemed to confuse the knight. (Grandpa Smedry has that effect on people.) However, once again, the knight simply shook his head and said, "Sorry."

Grandpa Smedry stepped back, annoyed, and I felt a twist of despair. I'd failed to help Bastille after all she'd gone through for me. She should have known that she shouldn't rely on me.

"How are you feeling, lad?" Grandpa Smedry asked.

I shrugged.

"Annoyed?" he prompted.

"Yeah."

"Frustrated?"

"A bit."

"Bitter?"

"You're not helping."

"I know I'm not. Angry?"

I didn't answer. The truth was, I *did* feel angry. At myself, mostly. For partying with Rodrayo and his friends while Bastille was in trouble. For forgetting about Mokia and its problems. For letting my grandfather down. It hadn't been that long ago that I'd always assumed that I'd let everyone down. I'd pushed people away before they could abandon me.

But working with Grandpa Smedry and the others had made me begin to feel that I *could* lead a normal life. Maybe I *didn't* have to alienate everyone. Maybe I *was* capable of having friendships, of having family, of . . .

There was a slight cracking sound.

"Oops!" Grandpa Smedry said in a loud voice. "Looks like you've gone and upset the boy!"

I started, looking down, realizing that I'd let my Talent crack the glass beneath my feet. Twin spiderwebs of lines crept from my shoes, marring the otherwise perfect crystal. I blushed, embarrassed.

The knights had grown pale. "Impossible!" one said.

"This crystal is supposed to be unbreakable!" the other said.

"My grandson," Grandpa Smedry said proudly. "He has the breaking Talent, you know. Upset him too much, and the entire floor could shatter. Actually, the entire castle could —"

"Get him out, then," one of the knights said, shooing me away like one might treat an unwanted puppy.

"What?" Grandpa Smedry said. "Antagonize him by throwing him out, and you could destroy the castle itself! We'll just have to see if he calms down. His Talent can be very unpredictable when he's emotional."

I could see what Grandpa Smedry was doing. I hesitated, then focused my power, trying to further crack the glass at my feet. It was an extremely foolhardy thing to do. That's what made it *exactly* the sort of plan Grandpa Smedry would come up with.

The spiderwebs at my feet grew larger. I steadied myself by touching the wall, and immediately created a ring of cracks around my hand.

"Wait!" one of the knights exclaimed. "I'll go in and ask if you can enter!"

Grandpa Smedry beamed. "What a nice fellow," he said, taking my arm, stopping me from breaking more. The knight opened the door, stepping inside.

"Did we really just *blackmail* a Knight of Crystallia?" I asked under my breath.

"Two of them, I believe," Grandpa Smedry said. "And it was really more 'intimidation' than it was 'blackmail.' Maybe with a twist of 'extortion.' It's always best to use the proper terminology!"

The knight returned, then — with a sigh — gestured for us to enter the chamber. We walked in eagerly.

And then Grandpa Smedry exploded.

CHAPTER 11

Okay, so he didn't really explode. I just wanted you to turn the page really fast.

You see, if you turn the pages quickly, you might rip one of them. If you do that, then — obviously — you'll want to go buy another copy of the book. Who wants one with a ripped page? Not you. You have refined tastes.

In fact, think of all the wonderful ways you can use this book. It will make an excellent coaster. You could also use it as building material. Or you could frame the pages as art. (After all, each page is a perfect work of art. Look at 56. Exquisite.)

Obviously, you need *lots* of copies. One isn't enough. Go buy more. Have you forgotten that you need to fight the Librarians?

Anyway, after getting done *not* exploding, Grandpa Smedry went into the chamber. I followed, expecting to find a courtroom. I was surprised to find only a simple wooden table with three knights sitting behind it. Bastille stood by the far wall, at attention, hands at her sides, staring straight ahead. The three knights at the table weren't even looking at her as they decided her punishment.

One of the knights was a masculine, burly man with an enormous chin. He was dangerous in an "I'm a knight, and I could totally kill you" sort of way.

Next to him was Bastille's mother, Draulin, who was dangerous in an "I'm Bastille's mother, and I could also kill you" sort of way.

The third one was an elderly, bearded knight who was dangerous in a "Stop playing your rap music so loud, you darn kids! Plus, I could kill you too" sort of way.

Judging by their expressions, they were not happy to see my grandfather and me. "Lord Smedry," the man with the chin said, "why have you interrupted these proceedings? You know you have no authority here."

"If I let that stop me, I'd never have any fun!" Grandpa Smedry said.

"This is *not* about fun, Lord Smedry," Bastille's mother said. "It's about justice."

"Oh, and since when has it been 'just' to punish someone for things that were not their fault?"

"We are not looking at fault," said the aged knight. "If a knight is incapable of protecting his or her charges, then that knight must be removed from his or her station. It is not young Bastille's fault if we promoted her too quickly and —"

"You didn't promote her too quickly," I snapped. "Bastille is the most amazing knight in your ranks."

"And you know much about the knights in our ranks, young Smedry?" the aged knight asked.

He was right. I felt a little foolish — but then when has *that* ever stopped a Smedry?

"No," I admitted. "But I do know that Bastille has done a fantastic job of protecting my grandfather and me. She's an excellent soldier — I saw her go head-to-head with one of the Scrivener's Bones and hold her own with only a dagger. I've seen her take down two Librarian thugs before I could even finish blinking."

"She lost her sword," Draulin said.

"So?" I demanded.

"It's the symbol of a Knight of Crystallia," Big Chin said.

"Well, get her another sword, then!" I snapped.

"It's not that easy," the old knight explained. "The fact that a knight is not capable of caring for her sword is very disturbing. We need to maintain quality in the order for the good of all nobility."

I stepped forward. "Did she tell you how the sword broke?"

"She was fighting Alivened," Draulin said. "She rammed it in one of their chests, then she was hit and knocked aside. When the Alivened was killed by falling through the floor, the sword was lost."

I glanced back at Bastille. She didn't meet my eyes.

"No," I said, looking back at them. "That's what happened, yes, but it's not what *happened*. It wasn't the fall, or even the death of the Alivened, and the sword wasn't just lost. It was destroyed. By me. My Talent."

The big-chinned knight gave a chuckle at that. "Lord Smedry," he said, "I understand that you are loyal and care for your friends, and I respect you for it. Good man! But you shouldn't make such wild exaggerations. Everyone knows that full Crystin shards are impervious to things like Oculator's Lenses and Smedry Talents!"

I stepped forward to the table. "Hand me your sword, then."

The knight started. "What?"

"Give it to me," I said, holding out a hand. "Let's see if it's impervious."

There was silence in the small glass chamber for a moment. The knight seemed incredulous. (Crystin don't let others hold their swords. Asking Big Chin to give me his was a little like asking the president to loan me his nuclear missile launching codes for the weekend.)

Still, backing down would make Big Chin look like he believed my claim. I could see the indecision in his eyes, his hand hovering toward the hilt of his weapon, as if to hand it over.

"Be careful, Archedis," Grandpa Smedry said quietly. "My grandson's Talent is not to be underestimated. The breaking Talent, by my estimation, hasn't been manifest this powerfully for centuries. Perhaps millennia."

The knight moved his hand away from the sword. "The breaking Talent," he said. "Well, perhaps it *is* possible for that to affect a Crystin sword."

Draulin pursed her lips, and I could tell that she wanted to object.

"Um," I said, glancing at my grandfather. He indicated that I should keep talking. "Anyway, I've come to speak at this trial, as is my right as a member of the Smedry clan."

"I believe you have been doing that already," Draulin said flatly. (Sometimes I can see where Bastille gets her snark.)

"Yes, well," I continued, "I want to vouch for Bastille's skill and cleverness. Without her intervention, both Grandpa Smedry and I would be dead. *You* probably would be too, Draulin. Let's not forget that you were captured by the very Librarian that Bastille defeated."

"I saw *you* defeat that Librarian, Lord Smedry," Draulin said. "Not my daughter."

"We did it together," I said. "As part of a plan we came up with as a team. You got your sword back only because Bastille and I retrieved it for you."

"Yes," said the elderly knight. "But then, that is part of the problem."

"It is?" I said. "Wounding Draulin's pride caused that much trouble?"

Draulin blushed — I felt pleased, though a little ashamed, for getting such a reaction out of her.

"It's more than that," Big Chin — Archedis — said. "Bastille held her mother's sword."

"She didn't have much choice," I said. "She was trying to save my life, and that of her mother — not to mention my father's life by association. Besides, she only picked it up for a short time."

"Regardless," Archedis said. "Bastille's use of the sword . . . interfered with it. It is more than tradition that keeps us from letting others hold our weapons."

"Wait," I said. "Does this have to do with those crystals in your necks?"

The three knights shared a look.

"We don't discuss these kinds of things with outsiders," the elderly knight said.

"I'm not an outsider," I said. "I'm a Smedry. Besides, I know most of it already." There were three kinds of Crystin shards — the ones that they made into swords, the ones they implanted in Crystin necks, and a third one Bastille hadn't wanted to talk about.

"You bond to those neck crystals," I said, pointing. "You bond to the swords too, don't you? Is that what this is all about? When Bastille picked up her mother's sword to fight Kilimanjaro, it interfered with the bond?"

"That's not *all* this is about," the oldest knight said.

"This is much bigger than that. What Bastille did in fighting with her mother's sword showed recklessness — just like losing her own sword did."

"So?" I demanded.

"So?" Draulin asked. "Young Lord Smedry, we are an order *founded* on the principle of keeping people like yourself alive. The kings, nobility, and particularly *Smedrys* of the Free Kingdoms seem to seek their own deaths with regularity. In order to protect them, the Knights of Crystallia must be constant and coolheaded."

"With all due respect, young Lord Smedry," the aged knight said, "it is our job to counteract your foolhardy nature, not encourage it. Bastille is not yet right for knighthood."

"Look," I said. "Somebody decided that she was worthy of being a knight. Maybe we should talk to them?"

"We *are* them," Archedis said. "We three elevated Bastille to knighthood six months ago, and are also the ones who chose her first assignment. That is why we are the ones who must face the sad task of stripping her knighthood from her. I believe it is time for us to vote."

"But — "

"Lord Smedry," Draulin said curtly. "You have had your say, and we suffered you. Have you anything more to say that will *productively* add to this argument?"

They all regarded me. "Would calling them idiots be productive?" I asked, turning toward my grandfather.

"Doubtful," he said, smiling. "You could try 'nigglenut,' since I bet they don't know the meaning. That probably wouldn't help much either."

"Then I'm done," I said, feeling even more annoyed than when I'd first entered the room.

"Draulin, your vote?" the aged knight — obviously in charge — said.

"I vote to strip knighthood from her," Draulin said. "And sever her from the Mindstone for one week to remove her taint from Crystin blades that do not belong to her."

"Archedis?" the elderly knight asked.

"The young Smedry's speech has moved me," the large-chinned knight said. "Perhaps we have been hasty. I vote to suspend knighthood, but not remove it. Bastille's taint of another's sword must be cleansed, but I believe one week to be too harsh. One day should suffice."

I didn't really know what that last part meant, but the big knight earned a few points in my book for his kindness.

"Then it is up to me," the aged knight said. "I will take the middle road. Bastille, we strip your knighthood from you, but will have another hearing in one week to reevaluate. You are to be severed from the Mindstone for two days. Both punishments are effective immediately. Report to the chamber of the Mindstone."

I glanced back at Bastille. Somehow I felt that decision wasn't in our favor. Bastille continued to stare straight ahead, but I could see lines of tension — even fear — in her face.

I won't let this happen! I thought, enraged. I gathered my Talent. They couldn't take her. I could stop them. I'd show them what it was like when my Talent broke *their* swords and —

"Alcatraz, lad," Grandpa Smedry said softly. "Privileges, such as our ability to visit Crystallia, are retained when they are not abused. I believe we have pushed our friends as far as they will go."

I glanced at him. Sometimes there was a surprising depth of wisdom in those eyes of his.

"Let it go, Alcatraz," he said. "We'll find another way to fight this."

The knights had stood and were making their way from

the room, likely eager to get away from my grandfather and me. I watched, helpless, as Bastille followed them. She shot me a glance as she left and whispered a single word. "Thanks."

Thanks, I thought. *Thanks for what? For failing?*

I was, of course, feeling guilty. Guilt, you may know, is a rare emotion that is much like an elevator made of Jell-O. (Both will let you down quite abruptly.)

"Come, lad," Grandpa Smedry said, taking my arm.

"We failed," I said.

"Hardly! They were ready to strip her knighthood completely. At least we've got a chance for her to get it back. You did well."

"A chance to get it back," I said, frowning. "But if the same people are going to vote again in a week, then what good have we done? They'll just vote to strip her knighthood completely."

"Unless we show them she deserves it," Grandpa said. "By, say, stopping the Librarians from getting that treaty signed and taking over Mokia?"

Mokia was important. But even if we *could* do what he said, and even if we *could* get Bastille involved, how was fighting a political battle going to prove anything to do with knighthood?

"What's a Mindstone?" I asked as we walked back to the Transporter chamber.

"Well," Grandpa Smedry said, "you're not supposed to know about that. Which, of course, makes it all the more fun to tell you. There are three kinds of Crystin shards."

"I know," I interjected. "They make swords from one type."

"Right," Grandpa Smedry said. "Those are special in that they're very resilient to Oculatory powers and things like Smedry Talents, which lets the Knights of Crystallia fight Dark Oculators. The second type of shards are the ones in their necks — the Fleshstones, they call them."

"Those give them powers," I said. "Make them better soldiers. But what's the third one?"

"The Mindstone," Grandpa Smedry said. "It is said to be a shard from the Worldspire itself, a single crystal that connects all the other Crystin shards. Even I don't know for certain what it does, but I think it connects all Crystin together, letting them draw upon the strength of other knights."

"And they're going to cut Bastille off from it," I said. "Maybe that will be a good thing. She'll be more her own person."

Grandpa Smedry eyed me. "The Mindstone doesn't make the knights all have a single mind, lad. It lets them share skills. If one of them knows how to do something, they all get a fraction of a tad of an iota better at that same thing."

We entered the room with the box, then stepped inside it; apparently, Grandpa Smedry had left instructions for the boxes to be swapped every ten minutes until we returned.

"Grandfather," I said. "My Talent. Is it as dangerous as you said back there?"

He didn't reply.

"In the tomb of Alcatraz the First," I said as the doors to our box closed, "the writing on the walls spoke of the breaking Talent. The writing . . . called it the 'Dark Talent' and implied it had caused the fall of the entire Incarna civilization."

"Others have held the breaking Talent, lad," Grandpa Smedry said. "None of them caused any civilizations to fall! Though they did knock down a wall or two."

His attempt at mirth seemed forced. I opened my mouth to ask more, but the doors to the box opened. Standing directly outside was Folsom Smedry in his red robes, Himalaya at his side.

"Lord Smedry!" Folsom said, looking relieved. "Finally!"

"What?" Grandpa Smedry said.

"You're late," Folsom said.

"Of course I am," Grandpa said. "Get on with it!"

"She's here."

"Who?"

"*Her,*" Folsom said. "She Who Cannot Be Named. She's in the keep, and she wants to talk to you."

CHAPTER 12

Right now, you should be asking yourself some questions. Questions like: "How is it possible that this book can be *so* awesome?" and "Why did the Librarian slip and fall down?" and "What exactly was it that exploded and made the *Hawkwind* crash in Chapter Two?"

Did you think I'd forgotten that last one? No, not at all. (The crash nearly killed me, after all.) I figured that the Librarians might be behind it, as everyone else assumed. But *why* had they done it? And, more important, *how*?

There just hadn't been time to ask those questions, important though they were. Too much was going on. We'll get to it, though.

(Also, the answer to the second question in the first paragraph is obvious. She fell because she was looking through the library's nonfriction section.)

We approached Keep Smedry's audience lounge, where

Sing — with his hefty Mokian girth — stood guard. It was time to confront She Who Cannot Be Named — the most dangerous Librarian in all of the Order of the Wardens of the Standard. I'd fought Blackburn, Dark Oculator, and felt the pain of his Torturer's Lens. I'd fought Kilimanjaro, of the Scrivener's Bones, with his blood-forged Lenses and terrible half-metal smile. Librarian hierarchs were not to be trifled with.

I tensed, entering the medium-sized castle chamber with Grandpa Smedry and Folsom, ready for anything. The Librarian, however, wasn't there. The only person in the room was a little old grandmother wearing a shawl and carrying an orange handbag.

"It's a trap!" I said. "They sent a grandmother as a decoy! Quickly, old lady. You're in great danger! Run for safety while we secure the area!"

The old lady met Grandpa Smedry's eyes. "Ah, Leavenworth. Your family is always such a delight!"

"Kangchenjunga Sarektjåkkå," Grandpa Smedry said, his voice uncharacteristically subdued. Almost cold.

"You always *were* the only one out here who could pro-nounce that correctly!" said Kagechech . . . Kachenjuaha . . . She Who Cannot Be Named. Her voice had a decidedly kindly tone to it. *This?* This was She Who Cannot Be Named? The most dangerous Librarian of all? I felt a little bit let down.

"Such a dear you are, Leavenworth," she continued.

Grandpa Smedry raised an eyebrow. "I can't say it's good to see you, Kangchenjunga, so instead — perhaps — I will say that it's *interesting* to see you."

"Does it have to be that way?" she asked. "Why, we're old friends!"

"Hardly. Why have you come here?"

The old grandmother sighed, then walked forward on shaky legs, back bowed with age, using a cane to walk. The room was carpeted with a large maroon rug, the walls bearing similar tapestries, along with several formal-looking couches for meeting with dignitaries. She didn't sit in one of these, however, she just walked up to my grandfather.

"You never *have* forgiven me for that little incident, have you?" the Librarian asked, fiddling in her handbag.

"Incident?" Grandpa Smedry said. "Kangchenjunga, I believe you left me dangling from a frozen mountain cliff, my foot tied to a slowly melting block of ice, my body strapped with bacon and stuck with a sign that read 'Free Wolf-chow.'"

She smiled wistfully. "Ah, now *that* was a trap. Kids these days don't know how to do it correctly." She reached into her handbag. I tensed, and then she pulled out what appeared to be a plate of chocolate chip cookies, wrapped in plastic wrap. She handed these to me, then patted me on the head. "What a pleasant lad," she said, then turned to my grandfather.

"You asked why I had come, Leavenworth," she said. "Well, we want the kings to know that we are serious about this treaty, and so I have come to speak before the final vote this evening."

I stared down at the cookies, expecting them to explode or something. Grandpa Smedry didn't seem worried — he kept his eyes focused directly on the Librarian.

"We won't let this treaty happen," Grandpa said.

The Librarian tsked quietly, shaking her head as she shuffled out of the room. "So unforgiving, you Smedrys. What can we do to show that we're sincere? What possible solution is there to all of this?"

She hesitated by the door, then turned and winked at us. "Oh, and *don't* get in my way. If you do, I'll have to rip out your entrails, dice them into little bits, then feed them to my goldfish. Toodles!"

I stared in shock. Everything about her screamed "kindly grandmother." She even smiled in a cute-old-lady sort of way when she mentioned our entrails, as if discussing a favored knitting project. She exited, and a couple of keep guards followed her.

Grandpa Smedry sat down on one of the couches, exhaling deeply, Folsom sitting next to him. Sing still stood by the door, looking disturbed.

"Well, then," Grandpa said. "My, my."

"Grandfather," I said, looking down at the cookies. "What should we do with these?"

"We probably shouldn't eat them," he said.

"Poison?" I asked.

"No. They'll spoil our dinner." He stopped, then shrugged. "But that's the Smedry way!" He slipped a cookie out and took a bite. "Ah, yes. As good as I remember. One of the nice things about facing off against Kangchenjunga is the treats. She's an excellent baker."

I noticed a motion to the side, and turned as Himalaya entered the room. "Is she gone?" the dark-haired former Librarian asked.

"Yes," Folsom said, standing up immediately.

"That woman is *dreadful*," Himalaya said, sitting down.

"Ten out of ten points for evilness," Folsom agreed.

I remained suspicious of Himalaya. She had stayed outside because she didn't want to face a former colleague. But that had left her unsupervised. What had she been doing? Planting a bomb, like the one that blew up the *Hawkwind*? (See, I told you I hadn't forgotten about that.)

"We need a plan," Grandpa Smedry said. "We only have a few hours until the treaty vote. There *has* to be a way to stop this!"

"Lord Smedry, I've been talking to the other nobility," Sing said. "It . . . doesn't look good. They're all so tired of war. They want it to end."

"I'll agree the war is terrible," Grandpa Smedry said. "But, Clustering Campbells, surrendering Mokia isn't the answer! We need to show them that."

Nobody responded. The five of us sat in the room for a time, thinking. Grandpa Smedry, Sing, and Folsom enjoyed the cookies, but I held off. Himalaya wasn't eating them either. If they *were* poisoned, then she would know.

A short time later, a servant entered. "Lord Smedry," the young boy said, "Crystallia is requesting a Swap Time."

"Approved," Grandpa Smedry said.

Himalaya took a cookie and finally ate one. *So much for*

that theory, I thought with a sigh. A short time later, Bastille walked in.

I stood up, shocked. "Bastille! You're here!"

She appeared dazed, like she'd just suffered a repeated beating to the face. She looked at me and seemed to have trouble focusing. "I . . ." she said. "Yes, I am."

That gave me chills. Whatever they'd done to her in Crystallia must have been horrible if it left her unable to make sarcastic responses to my dumb comments. Sing rushed to pull over a chair for her. Bastille sat, hands in her lap. She was no longer wearing the uniform of a Squire of Crystallia — she had on a generic brown tunic and trousers, like a lot of the people I'd seen in the city.

"Child," Grandpa Smedry said, "how do you feel?"

"Cold," she whispered.

"We're trying to think of a way to stop the Librarians from conquering Mokia, Bastille," I said. "Maybe . . . maybe you can help."

She nodded absently. How were we going to involve her in helping expose the Librarian plot — and thereby get her knighthood back — if she could barely talk?

Grandpa Smedry glanced at me. "What do you think?"

"I think I'm going to go break some crystal swords," I snapped.

"Not about Bastille, lad," Grandpa said. "I can assure you, we're all in agreement about how she's been treated. We've got larger problems right now."

I shrugged. "Grandpa, I don't know anything about politics back in the *Hushlands*, let alone the politics here in Nalhalla! I have no idea what to do."

"We can't just sit here!" Sing said. "My people are dying as we speak. If the other Free Kingdoms remove their support, Mokia won't have the supplies to keep fighting."

"Maybe . . . maybe I could look at the treaty?" Himalaya said. "If I read it over, perhaps I would see something that you Nalhallans haven't. Some trick the Librarians are pulling that we could show to the monarchs?"

"Excellent!" Grandpa Smedry said. "Folsom?"

"I'll take her to the palace," he said. "There's a public copy there we can read."

"Lord Smedry," Sing said, "I think that you should speak to the kings again."

"I've tried that, Sing!"

"Yes," the Mokian said, "but maybe you could address

them formally in session. Maybe . . . I don't know, maybe that will embarrass them in front of the crowds."

Grandpa Smedry frowned. "Well, yes. I'd rather do a daring infiltration, though!"

"There . . . aren't many places to infiltrate," Sing said. "The entire city is friendly toward us."

"Except that Librarian embassy," Grandpa Smedry said, eyes twinkling.

We sat for a moment, then glanced at Bastille. She was supposed to be the voice of reason, telling us to avoid doing things that were . . . well, stupid.

She just stared forward, though, stunned from what had been done to her.

"Blast," Grandpa Smedry said. "Somebody tell me that infiltrating the embassy is a terrible idea!"

"It's a terrible idea," I said. "I don't know why, though."

"Because there's not likely to be anything of use there!" Grandpa Smedry said. "They're too clever for that. If anything, they have a secret base somewhere in the city. That's where we'd need to infiltrate, but we don't have time to find it! Somebody tell me that I should just go speak to the kings again."

"Uh," Sing said, "didn't I just do that?"

"I need to hear it again, Sing," Grandpa Smedry said. "I'm old and stubborn!"

"Then, really, you should speak to the kings."

"Spoilsport," Grandpa Smedry muttered under his breath.

I sat back, thinking. Grandpa Smedry was right — there probably *was* a secret Librarian lair in the city. My bet was that we'd find it somewhere near where my mother vanished when I was trailing her.

"What are the Royal Archives?" I asked.

"They're not a library," Folsom said quickly.

"Yes, the sign said that," I replied. "But if they aren't a library, what are they?" (I mean, telling me what something *isn't* really wasn't all that useful. I could put out a blorgadet and hang a sign on it that said "Most certainly *not* a hippopotamus" and it wouldn't help. I'd also be lying, since "blorgadet" is actually Mokian for hippopotamus.)

Grandpa Smedry turned toward me. "The Royal Archives —"

"*Not* a library," Sing added.

"— are a repository for the kingdom's most important texts and scrolls."

"That, uh, sounds an *awful* lot like a library," I said.

"But it's not," Folsom said. "Didn't you hear?"

"Right . . ." I said. "Well, a repository for books —"

"Which is in no way a library," Grandpa Smedry said.

"— sounds like exactly the sort of place the Librarians would be interested in." I frowned in thought. "Are there books in the Forgotten Language in there?"

"I'd guess some," Grandpa Smedry said. "Never been in there myself."

"You haven't?" I asked, shocked.

"Too much like a library," Grandpa Smedry said. "Even if it isn't one."

You Hushlanders may be confused by statements like this. After all, Grandpa Smedry, Sing, and Folsom have all been presented as very literate fellows. They're academics — quite knowledgeable about what they do. How, then, have they avoided libraries and reading?

The answer is that they *haven't* avoided reading. They love books. However, to them, books are a little like teenage boys: Whenever they start congregating, they make trouble.

"The Royal Archives," I said, then quickly added, "and I know it's *not* a library. Whatever it is, that's where my mother was going. I'm sure of it. She has the Translator's

Lenses; she's trying to find something in there. Something important."

"Alcatraz, the place is *very* well guarded," Grandpa Smedry said. "I doubt even Shasta would be able to sneak in unseen."

"I still think we should visit," I said. "We can look and see if there's anything suspicious going on."

"All right," Grandpa Smedry said. "You take Bastille and Sing and go. I'll compose a stirring speech to give at the final proceedings this evening! Maybe if I'm lucky, someone will try to assassinate me during the speech. That would make it at least ten times more dramatic!"

"Grandpa," I said.

"Yes?"

"You're crazy."

"Thank you! All right, let's get moving! We have an entire continent to save!"

CHAPTER 13

People tend to believe what other people tell them. This is particularly true if the people who are telling the people the thing that they're telling them are people who have a college degree in the thing about which they are telling people. (Telling, isn't it?)

College degrees are very important. Without college degrees, we wouldn't know who was an expert and who wasn't. And if we didn't know who was an expert, we wouldn't know whose opinion was the most important to listen to.

Or at least that's what the experts want us to believe. Those who have listened to Socrates know that they're supposed to ask questions. Questions like "If all people are equal, then why is my opinion worth less than that of the expert?" or "If I like reading this book, then why should I let someone else tell me that I *shouldn't* like reading it?"

That isn't to say that I don't like critics. My cousin is one, and — as you have seen — he's a very nice fellow. All I'm saying is that you should question what others tell you, even if they have a college degree. There are a lot of people who might try to stop you from reading this book. They'll come up to you and say things like "Why are you reading that trash?" or "You should be doing your homework," or "Help me, I'm on fire!"

Don't let them distract you. It's of vital importance that you keep reading. This book is very, very important.

After all, it's about *me*.

"The Royal Archives," I said, looking up at the vast building in front of me.

"Not a library," Sing added.

"Thanks, Sing," I said dryly. "I'd almost forgotten."

"Glad to help!" he said as we walked up the steps. Bastille followed; she was still barely responsive. She'd come to us because she'd been kicked out of Crystallia. Getting cut off from the knights' magic rock also required a period of exile from their giant glass mushroom.

(Those of you in the Hushlands, I *dare* you to work that last sentence into a conversation. "By the way, Sally, did you know that getting cut off from the knights' magic rock also requires a period of exile from their giant glass mushroom?")

A dragon crawled along the sides of the castles above me, growling quietly to itself. The Royal Archives (not a library) looked a lot like a building out of Greek history, with its magnificent white pillars and marble steps. The only difference was that it had castlelike towers. In Nalhalla, *everything* has castle towers. Even the outhouses. (You know, in case someone tries to seize the throne.)

"It's been a long time since I've been here," Sing said, happily waddling beside me. It was good to spend time with the pleasant anthropologist again.

"You've been here before?" I asked.

Sing nodded. "During my undergraduate days, I had to do research on ancient weapons. This place has books you can't find anywhere else. I'm actually a little sad to be back."

"This place is that bad?" I asked as we entered the cavernous main room of the Royal Archives. I didn't see any books — it looked mostly empty.

"This place?" Sing asked. "Oh, I didn't mean the Royal Archives, which is not a library. I was talking about Nalhalla. I didn't get to do as much research in the Hushlands as I wanted! I was deeply engaged in a study on Hushlander transportation when your grandfather got me and we started our infiltration."

"It's really not that interesting there," I said.

"You just say that because you are accustomed to it!" Sing said. "Each day, something new and exciting happened! Right before we left, I finally managed to meet a real *cabdriver*! I had him drive me around the block, and while I was disappointed that we didn't get into a car wreck, I'm sure after a few more days I could have experienced one."

"Those are kind of dangerous, Sing."

"Oh, I was ready for danger," he said. "I made sure to wear safety goggles!"

I sighed, but made no other comment. Trying to curb Sing's love of the Hushlands was like . . . well, like kicking a puppy. A six-foot-eight, three-hundred-fifty-pound Hawaiian puppy. Who liked to carry guns.

"This place doesn't look all that impressive," I said, glancing about at the majestic pillars and enormous hallways. "Where are the books?"

"Oh, this isn't the archives," Sing said, pointing toward a doorway. "The archives are in there."

I raised an eyebrow and walked to the door, then pulled it open. Inside, I found an army.

There were a good fifty or sixty soldiers, all standing at attention in ranks, their metal helmets glistening in the lamplight. At the back of the room, there was a set of stairs leading down.

"Wow," I said.

"Why, young Lord Smedry!" a voice boomed. I turned and was surprised to see Archedis — the big-chinned Knight of Crystallia from Bastille's trial — walking toward me. "How surprising to see you here!"

"Sir Archedis," I said. "I could say the same of you, I guess."

"There are always two full knights on guard at the Royal Archives," Archedis said.

"Not a library," one of the soldiers added.

"I was just here overseeing a shift change," Archedis said, stepping up to me.

He was a lot more intimidating when standing. Silvery armor, rectangular face, a chin that could destroy small countries if it fell into the wrong hands. Sir Archedis was the type of knight that people stuck on recruitment posters.

"Well," I said. "We came to investigate the Royal Archives —"

"Not a library," Sir Archedis said.

"— because we think the Librarians might be interested in them."

"They're quite well protected," Archedis said in his deep voice. "A half platoon of soldiers and two Crystin! But I suppose it couldn't hurt to have an Oculator around too, particularly when there are Librarians in town!"

He glanced over my shoulder. "I see that you've brought young Bastille with you," he added. "Good job — keep her moving about and not wallowing in her punishment!"

I glanced back at Bastille. She'd focused on Sir Archedis, and I thought I was beginning to see some emotion return to her. Likely she was thinking about how much she'd like to ram something long and pointy into his chest.

"I'm sorry we had to meet under such poor circumstances, Lord Smedry," Archedis said to me. "I've been following your exploits."

"Oh," I said, flushing. "You mean the books?"

Archedis laughed. "No, no, your *real* exploits! The battle against Blackburn was reportedly quite impressive, and I would have liked to see that fight with the Alivened. I hear that you handled yourself quite well."

"Oh," I said, smiling. "Well, thanks."

"But tell me," he said, leaning down. "Did you *really* break a Crystin sword with that Talent of yours?"

I nodded. "Hilt came right off in my hand. I didn't realize it, but the problem was my emotion. I was so nervous that the Talent activated with a lot of power."

"Well, I guess I just have to take your word!" Archedis said. "Would you like a knight as guard for your person during this investigation?"

"No," I said. "I think we'll be fine."

"Very well, then," he said, slapping me on the back. (Side note: Getting slapped — even affectionately — on the back by someone wearing gauntlets is *not* comfortable.) "Carry on, and best of luck." He turned to the soldiers. "Let them pass and follow their orders! This is the heir of House Smedry!"

The soldiers, en masse, saluted. With that, Archedis marched out the door, armor clinking.

"I *like* that guy," I said after he was gone.

"Everyone does," Sing said. "Sir Archedis is one of the most influential knights in the order."

"Oh, I don't think *everyone* likes him," I said, glancing at Bastille. She was watching the doorway.

"He's amazing," she whispered, surprising me. "He's one of the reasons I decided to join."

"But he was one of the ones who voted to have you stripped of your rank!"

"He was the least harsh on me," Bastille said.

"Only because *I* convinced him to be."

She regarded me with an odd expression; it seemed that she was coming out of her funk a little bit. "I thought you liked him."

"Well, I do," I said.

Or at least I *had* liked him — right up until the point that Bastille had started talking about how wonderful he was. Now, quite suddenly, I became convinced that Sir Archedis was plain and dull-witted. I prepared to explain this to Bastille, but was interrupted as the soldiers began to make way for us to pass.

"Ah, nice," Sing said, walking forward. "Last time, I had to spend an hour appeasing their security requirements."

Bastille followed. She obviously hadn't recovered completely, even if she was a little more animated. We entered the stairwell, and for a brief moment I was reminded of the

Library of Alexandria, with its wraithlike Librarians and endless rows of dusty tomes and scrolls. It had been beneath the ground too.

The similarity soon ended. Not only was the Royal Archives *not* a library, but the stairwell didn't end in a strange teleporting darkness. Instead, it stretched on for a distance, dusty and dry. When we finally reached the bottom, we found the two Knights of Crystallia standing guard at another set of doors. They saluted, apparently recognizing Sing and me.

"How long will you need access, my lord?" one of the knights asked.

"Oh," I said. "Um, I'm not really sure."

"Check back with us in an hour, if you don't mind," said the other knight — a stout woman with blond hair.

"All right," I said.

With that, the two knights pushed open the doors, letting me, Sing, and Bastille into the archives. "Wow," I said. That just didn't seem to cover it. "*Wow,*" I repeated, this time with emphasis.

You're probably expecting a grand description here. Something impressive to depict the majestic collection of tomes that made up the archives.

That's because you misinterpreted my "wow." You see, like all alphabetically late palindromic exclamations, "wow" can be interpreted a lot of different ways. It's what we call "versatile," which is just another way of saying that it's a dumb thing to say.

After all, "wow" could mean "That's great!" Or it could mean "That's disturbing." It could also mean "Oh, hey, look, a dinosaur is about to eat me!" Or it could even mean "I just won the lottery, though I don't know what I'll do with all that money, seeing as how I'm in the stomach of a dinosaur."

(As a side note to this side note: As we found in book one, it is true that most dinosaurs are fine folk and not at all man-eaters. However, there are some notable exceptions, such as the Quesadilla and the infamous Brontësister.)

In my case, "wow" didn't mean any of these things. It meant something closer to: "This place is a total mess!"

"This place is a total mess!" I exclaimed.

"No need to repeat yourself," Bastille grumbled. (Bastille speaks fluent woweeze.)

Books were heaped like piles of scrap in an old, run-down junkyard. There were mountains of them, discarded, abused, and in total disarray. The cavern seemed to extend forever, and the piles of books formed mounds and hills, like sand dunes made from pages and letters and words. I glanced back at the knights guarding the doorway. "Is there some kind of organization to all of this?" I asked hopefully.

The knight paled in the face. "Organization? Like . . . a cataloging system?"

"Yeah," I said. "You know, so that we can find stuff easily?"

"That's what Librarians do!" the blond knight said.

"Great," I said. "Just great. Thanks anyway." I sighed, stepping away from the door, which the knights closed behind me. I grabbed a lamp off the wall. "Well, let's go investigate," I said to the others. "See if we can find anything suspicious."

We wandered the room, and I tried not to let my annoyance get the better of me. The Librarians had done some horrible things to the Free Kingdoms; it made sense that the Nalhallans would have an irrational fear of Librarian ways. However, I found it amazing that a people who loved learning so much could treat books in such a horrible manner. From the way the tomes were strewn, it seemed to me that their method of "archiving" books was to toss them into the storage chamber and forget about them.

The piles grew larger and more mountainous near the back of the chamber, as if they'd been systematically pushed there by some infernal, literacy-hating bulldozer. I stopped, hands on my hips. I had expected a museum, or at least a den filled with bookshelves. Instead, I'd gotten a teenage boy's bedroom.

"How could they tell if anything was missing?" I asked.

"They can't," Sing said. "They figure if nobody can get in to steal books, then they don't have to keep them counted or organized."

"That's stupid," I said, holding up my light. The chamber was longer than it was wide, so I could see the walls on either side of me. The place wasn't infinite, like the Library of Alexandria had seemed. It was essentially just one very big room filled with thousands and thousands of books.

I walked back down the pathway between the mounds. How could you tell if anything was suspicious about a place you'd never visited before? I was about to give up when I heard it. A sound.

"I don't know, Alcatraz," Sing was saying. "Maybe we —"

I held up a hand, quieting him. "Do you hear that?"

"Hear what?"

I closed my eyes, listening. Had I imagined it?

"Over there," Bastille said. I opened my eyes to find her pointing toward one of the walls. "Scraping sounds, like . . ."

"Like digging," I said, scrambling over a stack of books. I climbed up the pile, slipping on what appeared to be several volumes of the royal tax code, until I reached the top and could touch the wall. It was, of course, made of glass. I pressed an ear against it.

"Yeah," I said. "There are *definitely* digging sounds coming from the other side. My mother didn't sneak in here, she snuck into a nearby building! They're tunneling into the Royal Archives!"

"Not —" Sing began.

"Yes," I said, "it's *not a library*. I get it."

"Actually," he said, "I was going to say 'Not to disagree, Alcatraz, but it's impossible to break into this place.'"

"What?" I said, sliding back down the pile of books. "Why?"

"Because it's built out of Enforcer's Glass," Bastille said.

She was looking better, but still somewhat dazed. "You can't break that, not even with Smedry Talents."

I looked back at the wall. "I've seen impossible things happen. My mother has Translator's Lenses; there's no telling what she's learned from the Forgotten Language so far. Maybe they know a way to get through that glass."

"Possible," Sing said, scratching his chin. "Though, to be honest, if I were them, I'd just tunnel into the stairwell out there, then come through the door."

I glanced at the wall. That *did* seem likely. "Come on," I said, rushing over and pulling open the door. The two knights outside glanced in.

"Yes, Lord Smedry?" one asked.

"Someone may be trying to dig into the stairwell," I said. "Librarians. Get some more troops down here."

The knights looked surprised, but they obeyed my orders, one rushing up the stairs to do as commanded.

I looked back at Bastille and Sing, who still stood in the room. Soldiers weren't going to be enough — I wasn't just going to sit and wait to see what plot the Librarians were going to be putting into effect. Mokia was in trouble, and *I* had to help. That meant blocking what my mother and the others were doing, perhaps even exposing their double-dealing to the monarchs.

"We need to figure out what it is in here that my mother wants," I said, "then take it first."

Bastille and Sing looked at each other, then glanced back at the ridiculous number of books. I could read their thoughts in their expressions.

Find the thing my mother wanted? Out of this mess? How could anyone find *anything* in here?

It was then that I said something I never thought I'd hear myself say, no matter how old I grew.

"We need a Librarian," I declared. *"Fast."*

CHAPTER 14

Yes, you heard that right. I — Alcatraz Smedry — needed a Librarian.

Now, you may have gotten the impression that there are absolutely no uses for Librarians. I'm sorry if I implied that. Librarians are *very* useful. For instance, they are useful if you are fishing for sharks and need some bait. They're also useful for throwing out windows to test the effects of concrete impact on horn-rimmed glasses. If you have enough Librarians, you can build bridges out of them. (Just like witches.)

And, unfortunately, they are *also* useful for organizing things.

I hurried up the stairs with Sing and Bastille. We had to push our way past the soldiers who now lined the steps; the men and women held their swords, looking concerned. I'd sent a soldier with a message for my grandfather and another for my father, warning them of what we'd discovered. I'd also ordered one of the knights to send a contingent to search nearby buildings — maybe they'd be able to find the Librarian base and the other end of the tunnel. I wasn't counting on that happening, though. My mother wouldn't be caught so easily.

"We need to go *fast*," I said. "There's no telling when my mother will break into that chamber."

I still felt a little bit sick for needing the help of a Librarian. It was frustrating. Terribly frustrating. In fact, I don't think I can accurately — through text — show you just *how* frustrating it was.

But because I love you, I'm going to try anyway. Let's start by randomly capitalizing letters.

"We cAn SenD fOr a draGOn to cArry us," SinG saId As we burst oUt oF the stAirWeLL and ruSHED tHrough ThE roOm aBovE.

"ThAT wILl taKe tOO Long," BaStiLlE saiD.

"We'Ll haVe To graB a VeHiCle oFf thE STrEet," I sAid.

(You know what, that's not nearly frustrating enough. I'm going to have to start adding in random punctuation marks too.)

We c!RoS-Sed thrOu?gH t%he Gra##ND e`nt<Ry>WaY at "A" de-aD Ru)n. OnC$e oUts/iDE, I Co*Uld sEe T^haT the suN wa+S nEar to s=Ett=ING — it w.O.u.l.d Onl>y bE a co@uPle of HoU[rs unTi^L the tR}e}atY RATiF~iCATiON ha,pPenEd. We nEeDeD!! to bE QuicK?.?

UnFOrTu()nAtelY, tHE!re weRe no C?arriA-ges on tHe rOa^D for U/s to cOmMan><dEer. Not a ON~e~. THerE w+eRe pe/\Ople wa|lK|Ing aBoUt, BU?t no caRr#iaGes.

(Okay, you know what? That's not frustrating enough either. Let's start replacing some random vowels with the letter Q.)

I lqOk-eD abO!qT, dE#sPqrA#te, fRq?sTr/Ated (like you, hopefully), anD aNn|qYeD. Jq!St eaR&lIer, tHqr^E hq.d BeeN DoZen!S of cq?RrIqgEs on The rQA!d! No-W tHqRe wA=Sn't a SqnGl+e oN^q.

"ThE_rQ!" I eXclai$mqd, poIntIng. Mqv=Ing do~Wn th_e RqaD! a shoRt diStq++nCe aWay <wAs> a sTrANgq gLaSs cqnTrAPtion. I waSN't CqrTain What it </wAs>, bUt It w!qs MoV?ing — aND s%qmewhat quIc:=)Kly. "LeT's G_q gRA?b iT!"

(Okay, you know how frustrated you are trying to read

that? Well, that's about *half* as frustrated as I was at having to go get a Librarian to help me. Aren't you happy I let you experience what I was feeling? That's the sign of excellent storytelling: writing that makes the reader have the same emotions as the characters. You can thank me later.)

We rushed up to the thing walking down the road. It was a glass animal of some sort, a little like the *Hawkwind* or the *Dragonaut*, except instead of flying, it was walking. As we rounded it, I got a better view.

I froze in place on the street. "A *pig*?"

Sing shrugged. Bastille, however, rushed toward the pig in a determined run. She looked less dazed, though she still had a very . . . worn-out cast to her. Her eyes were dark and puffy, her face haggard and exhausted. I jogged after her. As we approached the enormous pig, a section of glass on its backside slid away, revealing someone standing inside.

I feel the need to pause and explain that I don't approve of potty humor in the least. There has already been far too much of it in this book, and — trifecta or not — it's just not appropriate. Potty humor is the literary equivalent of potato chips and soda. Appealing, perhaps, but at the same time, dreadful and in poor taste. I will have you know that

I don't stand for such things and — as in the previous volumes of my narrative — intend to hold this story to rigorous quality standards.

"Farting barf-faced poop!" a voice exclaimed from inside the pig's butt.

(Sigh. Sorry. At least that's another great paragraph to try working into a random conversation.)

The man standing in the pig's posterior was none other than Prince Rikers Dartmoor, Bastille's brother, son of the king. He still wore his royal blue robes, his red baseball cap topping a head of red hair.

"Excuse me?" I said, stopping short outside the pig. "What was that you said, Your Highness?"

"I hear that Hushlanders like to use synonyms for excrement as curses!" the prince said. "I was trying to make you feel at home, Alcatraz! What in the world are you doing in the middle of the street?"

"We need a ride, Rikers," Bastille said. "*Fast.*"

"Explosive diarrhea!" the prince exclaimed.

"And for the last time, *stop* trying to talk like a Hushlander. It makes you sound like an idiot." She jumped up into the pig, then extended a hand to help me up.

I smiled, taking her hand.

"What?" she asked.

"Nice to see you're feeling better."

"I feel terrible," she snapped, sliding on her dark sun-glasseslike Warrior's Lenses. "I can barely concentrate, and I've got this horrible buzzing in my ears. Now shut up and climb in the pig's butt."

I did as ordered, letting her pull me up. Doing so was harder for her than it would have been previously — being disconnected from the Mindstone must have taken away some of her abilities — but she was still far stronger than any thirteen-year-old girl had a right to be. The Warrior's Lenses probably helped; they're one of the few types of Lenses that anyone can wear.

Bastille helped Sing up next as the prince rushed through the glass pig — which had a very nice, lush interior — calling for his driver to turn around.

"Uh, where are we going on our amazing adventure?" the prince called.

Amazing adventure? I thought. "To the palace," I called. "We need to find my cousin Folsom."

"The palace?" the prince said, obviously disappointed — for him, at least, that was a fairly mundane location. He called out the order anyway.

The pig started to move again, tromping down the street. The pedestrians apparently knew to stay out of its way, and despite its large size, it made very good time. I sat down on one of the regal red couches, and Bastille sat next to me, exhaling and closing her eyes.

"Does it hurt?" I asked.

She shrugged. She's good at the tough-girl act, but I could tell that the severing still bothered her deeply.

"Why do we need Folsom?" she asked, eyes still closed, obviously trying to distract me from asking after her.

"He'll be with Himalaya," I said, then realized that Bastille had never met the Librarian. "She's a Librarian who supposedly defected to our side six months back. I don't think she's to be trusted, though."

"Why?"

"Folsom stays suspiciously close to her," I said. "He rarely lets her out of his sight — I think he's worried that she's really a Librarian spy."

"Great," Bastille said. "And we're going to ask *her* for help?"

"She's our best bet," I said. "She is a fully trained Librarian — if anyone can sort through that mess in the Royal Archives —"

"Not a library!" Rikers called distantly from the front of the pig.

"— it will be a Librarian. Besides, maybe if she *is* a spy, she'll know what the Librarians are looking for, and we can force it out of her."

"So, your brilliant plan is to go to someone you suspect of being our enemy, then bring her into the very place that the Librarians are trying to break into."

"Er . . . yes."

"Wonderful. Why do I feel that I'm going to end this ridiculous fiasco wishing I'd just given up my knighthood and become an accountant instead?"

I smiled. It felt *good* to have Bastille back. It was hard for me to feel too impressed by my own fame with her there pointing out the holes in my plans.

"You don't really mean that, do you?" I asked. "About quitting the knighthood?"

She sighed, opening her eyes. "No. As much as I hate to admit it, my mother was right. I'm not only good at this, but I enjoy it." She looked at me, meeting my eyes. "Somebody set me up, Alcatraz. I'm convinced of it. They *wanted* me to fail."

"Your . . . mother was the one who voted most harshly against your reinstatement."

Bastille nodded, and I could see that she was thinking the same thing that I was.

"We have quite the parents, don't we?" I asked. "My father ignores me; my mother married him just to get his Talent."

Marry a Smedry, and you got a Talent. Apparently, it didn't matter if you were a Smedry by blood or by marriage: A Smedry was a Smedry. The only difference was that in the case of a marriage, the spouse got their husband's or wife's same Talent.

"My parents aren't like that," Bastille said fiercely. "They're good people. My father is one of the most respected and popular kings Nalhalla has ever known."

"Even if he is giving up on Mokia," Sing said quietly from his seat across from us.

"He *thinks* he's doing the best thing," Bastille said. "How would you like to have to decide whether to end a war — and save thousands of lives — or keep fighting? He sees a chance for peace, and the people *want* peace."

"My people want peace," Sing said. "But we want freedom more."

Bastille fell silent. "Anyway," she finally said, "assuming my mother *was* the one to set me up, I can see exactly why she'd do it. She worries about showing favoritism toward me. She feels she needs to be extra hard on me, which is why she'd send me on such a difficult mission. To see if I failed, and therefore needed to go back into training. But she *does* care for me. She just has strange ways of showing it."

I sat back, thinking about my own parents. Perhaps Bastille could come up with good motives for hers, but they were a noble king and a brave knight. What did I have? An egotistical rock-star scientist and an evil Librarian who even other *Librarians* didn't seem to like very much.

Attica and Shasta Smedry were not like Bastille's parents. My mother didn't care about me — she'd married only to get the Talent. And my father obviously didn't want to spend any time with me.

No wonder I turned out like I did. There is a saying in the Free Kingdoms: "A cub's roar is an echo of the bear."

It's a little bit like one we use in the Hushlands: "The apple doesn't fall far from the tree." (It figures that the Librarian version would use apples instead of something cool, like bears.)

I'm not sure if I ever had a chance to be anything *but* the selfish jerk I became. Despite Grandpa Smedry's chastisement, I still longed for the fleeting satisfaction of fame. It had been really nice to hear people talk about how great I was.

My taste of fame sat in me like a corrupt seed, blackened and putrid, waiting to sprout forth slimy dark vines.

"Alcatraz?" Bastille asked, elbowing me.

I blinked, realizing that I'd zoned out. "Sorry," I mumbled.

She nodded to the side. Prince Rikers was approaching. "I called ahead, and Folsom isn't at the palace," he said.

"He isn't?" I asked, surprised.

"No, the servants said that he and a woman looked over the treaty, then left. But never fear! We can continue our quest, for the servant said that we could find Folsom in the Royal Gardens —"

"*Not* a park," Sing said. "Or, er, never mind."

"— across the street."

"All right," I said. "What's he doing in the gardens?"

"Something terribly exciting and important, I'd guess," Rikers said. "Eldon, take notes!"

A servant in a scribe's robes appeared from a nearby room, as if from nowhere, with a notepad. "Yes, my lord," the man said, scribbling.

"This will make an excellent book," Rikers said, sitting down.

Bastille just rolled her eyes.

"So, wait," I said. "You called ahead? How'd you do that?"

"Communicator's Glass," Rikers said. "Lets you talk with someone across a distance."

Communicator's Glass. However, something about that bothered me. I reached into my pocket, pulling out my Lenses. I'd once had a pair of Lenses that let *me* communicate across a distance. I didn't have them anymore — I'd given them back to Grandpa Smedry. I did have the new set of Disguiser's Lenses, though. What about the power they gave me? If I was thinking about someone, I could make myself look like them. . . .

(By the way, yes, this *is* foreshadowing. However, you'll

need to have read the previous two books in the series to figure out what's going on. So if you haven't read them, then too bad for you!)

"Wait," Bastille said, pointing at the Truthfinder's Lens in my hand. "Is that the one you found in the Library of Alexandria?"

"Yeah. Grandpa figured out that it's a Truthfinder's Lens."

She perked up. "*Really?* Do you know how rare those are?"

"Well . . . to be honest, I kind of wish that it could blow things up."

Bastille rolled her eyes. "You wouldn't know a useful Lens if you cut your finger on it, Smedry."

She had a point. "You know a lot more about Lenses than I do, Bastille," I admitted. "But I think there's something odd about all of this. Smedry Talents, the Oculator's Lenses, brightsand . . . it's all connected."

She eyed me. "What are you talking about?"

"Here, let me show you." I tucked my Lenses away, standing up and scanning the chamber, looking for a likely candidate. On one wall, there was a small shelf with some glass equipment on it. "Your Highness, what's that?"

Prince Rikers turned. "Ah! My new silimatic phonograph! Haven't hooked it up yet, though."

"Perfect," I said, walking over and picking up the glass box; it was about the size of a briefcase.

"That won't work, Alcatraz," the prince said. "It needs a silimatic power plate or some brightsand to —"

I channeled power into the glass. Not breaking power from my Talent, but the same "power" I used to activate Lenses. Early on, I had simply needed to touch Lenses to power them; now I was learning to control myself so that I didn't activate them unintentionally.

Either way, the box started playing music — a peppy little symphony. It's a good thing Folsom wasn't there, otherwise he would have begun to "dance."

"Hey, how'd you do that?" Prince Rikers asked. "Amazing!"

Bastille regarded me quizzically. I set the music box down, and it continued to play for a time, powered by the charge I'd given it.

"I'm starting to think that Oculatory Lenses and regular technological glass might just be the same thing."

"That's impossible," she said. "If that were so, then you could power Oculator's Lenses with brightsand."

200

"You can't?"

She shook her head.

"Maybe it's not concentrated enough," I said. "You *can* power the Lenses with Smedry blood, if you forge them using it."

"Ick," she noted. "It's true. But ick anyway."

"Ah, here we are!" Rikers said suddenly, standing up as the pig slowed.

I shot Bastille a look. She shrugged; we'd discuss this more later. We stood and joined Rikers, looking out the window (or, well, the *wall*) at the approaching gardens. My sense of urgency returned. We needed to grab Himalaya and get back to the Royal, nonlibrary Archives.

Rikers pulled a lever, and the back of the pig unfolded, forming steps. Bastille and I rushed out, Sing hustling along behind. The Royal Gardens were a large, open field of grass dotted occasionally by beds of flowers. I scanned the green, trying to locate my cousin. Of course, Bastille found him first.

"There," she said, pointing. Squinting, I could see that Folsom and Himalaya were sitting on a blanket, enjoying what appeared to be a picnic.

"Wait here!" I called to Sing and Rikers as Bastille and I

crossed the springy grass, passing families enjoying the afternoon and kids playing.

"What in the world are those two doing?" I asked, looking at Folsom and Himalaya.

"Uh, I think that's called a picnic, Smedry," Bastille said flatly.

"I know, but why would Folsom take an enemy spy on a picnic? Perhaps he's trying to get her to relax so he can mine her for information."

Bastille regarded the two of them, who sat on the blanket enjoying their meal. "So, wait," she said as we rushed forward. "They're always together?"

"Yeah," I said. "He's been watching her like a hawk. He's always looking at her."

"You'd say he's been spending a lot of time with her?"

"A *suspicious* amount of time."

"Hanging out at restaurants?"

"Ice cream parlors," I said. "He claims to be showing her around so that she'd get used to Nalhallan customs."

"And you think he's doing this because he suspects her of being a spy," Bastille said, voice almost amused.

"Well, why else would he —"

I froze, stopping on the grass. Just ahead, Himalaya laid her hand on Folsom's shoulder, laughing at something he'd said. He regarded her, seeming transfixed by her face. He seemed to be enjoying himself, as if . . .

"Oh," I said.

"Boys are such idiots," Bastille said under her breath, moving on.

"How was I supposed to know they were in love!" I snapped, rushing up to her.

"Idiot," she repeated.

"Look, she *could* still be a spy. Why, maybe she's seducing Folsom to get at his secrets!"

"Seductions don't look so cutesy," Bastille said as we approached their blanket. "Anyway, there's a simple method to find out. Pull out that Truthfinder's Lens."

Hey, that's a good idea, I thought. I fumbled, pulling out the Lens and looking through it toward the Librarian.

Bastille marched right up to the blanket. "You're Himalaya?" she asked.

"Why, yes," the Librarian said. As I looked through the Lens, her breath seemed to glow like a white cloud. I assumed that meant she was telling the truth.

"Are you a Librarian spy?" Bastille asked. (She's like that, blunter than a rock and twice as ornery.)

"What?" Himalaya said. "No, of course not!"

Her breath was white.

I turned to Bastille. "Grandpa Smedry warned that Librarians were good at saying half-truths, which might get them around my Truthfinder's Lens."

"Are you saying half-truths?" Bastille said. "Are you trying to fool that Lens, trick us, seduce this man, or do anything like that?"

"No, no, no," Himalaya said, blushing.

Bastille looked at me.

"Her breath is white," I said. "If she's lying, she's doing a really great job of it."

"Good enough for me," Bastille said, pointing. "You two, get in the pig. We're on a tight schedule."

They jumped to their feet, not even asking questions. When Bastille gets that tone in her voice, you do what she says. For the first time, I realized where Bastille's ability to order people about might have come from. She was a princess — she'd probably spent her entire childhood giving commands.

By the First Sands, I thought. *She's a* princess.

"All right," Bastille said. "We've got your Librarian, Smedry. Let's hope she can actually help."

We headed back to the pig, and I eyed the setting sun. Not much time left. This next part was going to have to go quickly. (I suggest you take a deep breath.)

CHAPTER 15

Humans are funny things. From what I've seen, the more we agree with someone, the more we like listening to them. I've come up with a theory. I call it the macaroni and cheese philosophy of discourse.

I love macaroni and cheese. It's amazing. If they serve food in heaven, I'm certain mac and cheese graces each and every table. If someone wants to sit and talk to me about how good mac and cheese is, I'll talk to them for hours. However, if they want to talk about fish sticks, I generally stuff them in a cannon and launch them in the general direction of Norway.

That's the wrong reaction. I *know* what mac and cheese tastes like. Wouldn't it be more useful for me to talk to someone who likes something else? Maybe understanding what other people like about fish sticks could help me understand how they think.

A lot of the world doesn't think this way. In fact, a lot of people think that if they like mac and cheese rather than fish sticks, the best thing to do is *ban* fish sticks.

That would be a tragedy. If we let people do things like this, eventually we'd end up with only one thing to eat. And it probably wouldn't be mac and cheese *or* fish sticks. It'd probably be something that *none* of us likes to eat.

You want to be a better person? Go listen to someone you disagree with. Don't argue with them, just *listen*. It's remarkable what interesting things people will say if you take the time to not be a jerk.

We dashed from the giant glass pig like deployed soldiers, then stormed up the steps to the Royal Archives. (Go ahead, say it with me. I know you want to.)

Not a library.

Bastille in her Warrior's Lenses was the fastest, of course, but Folsom and Himalaya kept up. Sing was in the rear, right beside . . .

"Prince *Rikers*?" I said, freezing in place. I'd assumed that the prince would remain with his vehicle.

"Yes, what?" the prince said, stopping beside me, turning and looking back.

"Why are you here?" I said.

"I finally have a chance to see the famous Alcatraz Smedry in action! I'm not going to miss it."

"Your Highness," I said, "this might be dangerous."

"You really think so?" he asked excitedly.

"What's going on?" Bastille said, rushing back down the steps. "I thought we were in a hurry."

"He wants to come," I said, gesturing.

She shrugged. "We can't really stop him — he's the crown prince. That kind of means he can do what he wants."

"But what if he gets killed?" I asked.

"Then they'll have to pick a new crown prince," Bastille snapped. "Are we going or not?"

I sighed, glancing at the red-haired prince. He was smiling in self-satisfaction.

"Great," I muttered, but continued up the stairs. The prince rushed beside me. "By the way," I said. "Why a *pig*?"

"Why," he said, surprised, "I heard that in the Hushlands, it is common for tough guys to ride hogs."

I groaned. "Prince Rikers, 'hog' is another word for a motorcycle."

"Motorcycles look like pigs?" he asked. "I never knew that!"

"You know what, never mind," I said. We rushed into the room with the soldiers; it looked like the knights had sent for reinforcements. There were a lot of them on the stairs too. I felt good knowing they were there in case the Librarians *did* break into the Royal Archives.

"Not a library," Sing added.

"What?" I asked.

"Just thought you might be thinking about it," Sing said, "and figured I should remind you."

We reached the bottom. The two knights had taken up guard positions inside the room, and they saluted the prince as we entered.

"Any Librarians?" I asked.

"No," the blond knight said, "but we can still hear the scrapings. We have two platoons on command here, and two more searching nearby buildings. So far, we've not discovered anything — but we'll be ready for them if they break into the stairwell!"

"Excellent," I said. "You should wait outside, just in case." I didn't want them to see what was about to happen. It was embarrassing.

They left and closed the door. I turned to Himalaya. "All right," I said. "Let's do it."

She looked confused. "Do what?"

Oh, right, I thought. We'd never actually explained why we needed her. "Somewhere in this room are some books the Librarians really want," I said. "Your former friends are tunneling in here right now. I need you to . . ."

I could see Bastille, Folsom, and Sing cringe as I prepared to say it.

". . . I need you to *organize* the books in here."

Himalaya paled. "What?"

"You heard me right."

She glanced at Folsom. He looked away.

"You're testing me," she said, forming fists. "Don't worry, I can resist it. You don't need to do this."

"No, really," I said, exasperated. "I'm not testing you. I just need these books to have some kind of order."

She sat down on a pile. "But . . . but I'm recovering! I've been clean for months now! You can't ask me to go back, you *can't.*"

"Himalaya," I said, kneeling beside her. "We really, really need you to do this."

She started trembling, which made me hesitate.

"I —"

She stood and fled the room, tears in her eyes. Folsom

rushed after her, and I was left kneeling, feeling horrible. Like I'd just told a little girl that her kitten was dead. Because I'd run it over. And that I'd also eaten it.

And that it had tasted really bad.

"Well, that's that, then," Bastille said. She sat down on a pile of books. She was starting to look haggard again. We'd kept her distracted for a time, but the severing was still weighing on her.

I could still hear the scraping sounds, and they were getting louder. "All right, then," I said, taking a deep breath. "We're going to have to destroy them."

"What?" Sing asked. "The books?"

I nodded. "We *can't* let my mother get what she wants. Whatever it is, I'll bet it involves Mokia. This is the only thing I can think of — I doubt we can move these books out in time." I looked toward the mounds. "We're going to have to burn them."

"We don't have the authority for that," Bastille said tiredly.

"Yes," I said, turning toward Prince Rikers. "But I'll bet that he does."

The prince looked up — he'd been poking through a pile of books, probably looking for fantasy novels. "What's this?" he asked. "I have to say, this adventure hasn't been very exciting. Where are the explosions, the rampaging wombats, the space stations?"

"This is what a real adventure is like, Prince Rikers," I said. "We need to burn these books so the Librarians don't get them. Can you authorize that?"

"Yes, I suppose," he said. "A bonfire might be exciting."

I walked over and grabbed one of the lamps off the walls. Bastille and Sing joined me, looking at the books as I prepared to begin the fire.

"This feels wrong," Sing said.

"I know," I said. "But what does anyone care about these books? They just stuffed them in here. I'll bet people rarely even come look at them."

"I did," Sing said. "Years back. I can't be the only one. Besides, they're *books*. Knowledge. Who knows what we might lose? There are books in here that are so old, they might be the only copies in existence outside of the ones at the Library of Alexandria."

I stood with the fire in my hand. Now, I hadn't meant this to be a metaphor for anything — I'm simply relating what happened. It *did* seem like the right thing to do. And yet, it also felt like the *wrong* thing too. Was it better to burn the books and let nobody have the knowledge, or take the chance that the Librarians would get them?

I knelt and put the lamp toward a stack of books, its flame flickering.

"Wait," Bastille said, kneeling beside me. "You have to turn it to 'burn.'"

"But it's already burning," I said, confused.

"Not that argument again," she said, sighing. (Go read book one.) "Here." She touched the glass of the lamp, and the flame seemed to pulse. "It's ready now."

I took a deep breath, then — hand trembling — lit the first book on fire.

"Wait!" a voice called. "Don't do it!"

I spun to see Himalaya standing in the doorway, Folsom at her side. I looked back at the books desperately; the flame was already spreading.

Then, fortunately, Sing tripped. His enormous Mokian bulk smashed onto the pile of books, his gut completely extinguishing the flames. A little trickle of smoke curled out from underneath him.

"Whoops," he said.

"No," Himalaya said, striding forward. "You did the right thing, Sing. I'll do it. I'll organize them. Just . . . just don't hurt them. Please."

I stepped back as Folsom helped Sing to his feet. Himalaya knelt by the pile that had almost gone up in flames. She touched one of the books lovingly, picking it up with her delicate fingers.

"So . . . uh," she said, "what order do you want? Reverse timeshare, where the books are organized by the minute when they were published? Marksman elite, where we organize them by the number of times the word 'the' is used in the first fifty pages?"

"I think a simple organization by topic will do," I said. "We need to find the ones about Oculators or Smedrys or anything suspicious like that."

Himalaya caressed the book, feeling its cover, reading the spine. She carefully placed it next to her, then picked up another. She placed that one in another pile.

This is going to take forever, I thought with despair.

Himalaya grabbed another book. This time, she barely glanced at the spine before setting it aside. She grabbed another, then another, then another, moving more quickly with each volume.

She stopped, taking a deep breath. Then she burst into motion, her hands moving more quickly than I could track. She seemed to be able to identify a book simply by touching it, and knew exactly where to place it. In mere seconds, a small wall of books was rising around her.

"A little help, please!" she called. "Start moving the stacks over, but don't let them get out of order!"

Sing, Folsom, Bastille, and I hurried forward to help. Even the prince went to work. We rushed back and forth, moving books where Himalaya told us, struggling to keep up with the Librarian.

She was almost superhuman in her ability to organize — a machine of identification and order. Dirty, unkempt piles disappeared beneath her touch, transformed into neat stacks, the dust and grime cleaned from them in a single motion of her hand.

Soon Folsom got the idea to recruit some of the soldiers to help. Himalaya sat in the center of the room like some multiarmed Hindu goddess, her hands a blur. We brought her stacks of books and she organized them in the blink of an eye, leaving them grouped by subject. She had a serene smile on her face. It was the smile my grandfather had when he spoke of an exciting infiltration, or the way Sing looked when he spoke of his cherished antique weapons collection. It was the look of someone doing work they perfectly and truly enjoyed.

I rushed forward with another stack of books. Himalaya snatched them without looking at me, then threw them into piles like a dealer dealing cards.

Impressive! I thought.

"All right, I have to say it," Himalaya said as she worked. Soldiers clinked in their armor, rushing back and forth, delivering stacks of unorganized books to her feet, then taking away the neatly organized ones she placed behind her.

"What is wrong with you Free Kingdomers?" she demanded, ranting as if to nobody in particular. "I mean, I left the Hushlands because I disagreed with the way the Librarians were keeping information from the people.

"But why is it bad to organize? Why do you have to treat books like this? What's wrong with having a little order? You Free Kingdomers claim to like things loose and free, but if there are never any rules, there is chaos. Organization is *important*."

I set down my stack of books, then rushed back.

"Who knows what treasures you could have lost here?" she snapped, arms flying. "Mold can destroy books. Mice can chew them to bits. They need to be cared for, *treasured*. Somebody needs to keep track of what you have so that you can appreciate your own collection!"

Folsom stepped up beside me, his brow dripping with sweat. He watched Himalaya with adoring eyes, smiling broadly.

"Why did I have to give up who I was?" the Librarian ranted. "Why can't I be me, but also be on your side? I don't want to stifle information, but I do want to organize it! I don't want to rule the world, but I do want to bring it order! I don't want everything to be the same, but I *do* want to understand!"

She stopped for a moment. "I am a *good* Librarian!" she declared in a triumphant voice, grabbing a huge stack of unorganized books. She shook them once, like one might a pepper shaker, and somehow the books all aligned in order by subject, size, and author.

"*Wow,*" Folsom breathed.

"You really *do* love her," I said.

Folsom blushed, looking at me. "Is it that obvious?"

It hadn't been to me. But I smiled anyway.

"These last six months have been amazing," he said, getting that dreamy, disgusting tone to his voice that love-sick people often use. "I started out just watching to see if she was a spy, but after I determined that she was safe . . . well, I wanted to keep spending time with her. So I offered to coach her on Nalhallan customs."

"Have you told her?" I asked, soldiers bustling around me, carrying stacks of books.

"Oh, I couldn't do that," Folsom said. "I mean, look at her. She's amazing! I'm just a regular guy."

"A regular guy?" I asked. "Folsom, you're a Smedry. You're nobility!"

"Yeah," he said, looking down. "But I mean, that's just a name. I'm a boring person, when you get down to it. Who thinks a critic is interesting?"

I resisted pointing out that Librarians weren't exactly known for being the most exciting people either.

"Look," I said. "I don't know a lot about things like this, but it seems to me that if you love her, you should say so. I —"

At that moment, Prince Rikers walked up. "Hey, look!"

he said, proffering a book. "They have one of my novels in here! Preserved for all of posterity. The music even still works. See!"

He opened the cover.

And so, of course, Folsom punched me in the face.

CHAPTER 16

NOW, I would like to make it clear that violence is rarely the best solution to problems.

For instance, the next time you get attacked by a group of angry ninjas, one solution would be to kick the lead ninja, steal his katana, and proceed to slay the rest of the group in an awesome display of authorial fury. While this might be fulfilling — and a little bit fun — it would also be rather messy, and would earn you the ire of an entire ninja clan. They'd send assassins after you for the rest of your life. (Having to fight off a ninja in the middle of a date can be quite embarrassing.)

So instead of fighting, you could bribe the ninjas with soy sauce, and then send them to attack your siblings instead. That way, you can get rid of some unwanted soy sauce. See how easy it is to avoid violence?

Now, there *are* some occasions when violence is

appropriate. Usually, those are occasions when you want to beat the tar out of somebody. Unfortunately, "somebody" at this moment happened to be me. Folsom's punch was completely unexpected, and it hit me full in the face.

Right then, I realized something quite interesting: That was the first time I'd ever been punched. It was a special moment for me. I'd say it was a little like being kicked, only with more knuckles and a hint of lemon.

Maybe the lemon part was just my brain short-circuiting as I was tossed backward onto the chamber's glass floor. The blow left me dazed, and by the time I finally shook myself out of it, the scene in front of me was one of total chaos.

The soldiers were trying to subdue Folsom. They didn't want to hurt him, as he was a nobleman; they were forced to try to grab him and hold him down. It wasn't working very well. Folsom fought with a strange mixture of terrified lack of control and calculated precision. He was like a puppet being controlled by a kung fu master. Or maybe vice versa. A trite melody played in the background — my theme music, apparently.

Folsom moved among the soldiers in a blur of awkward (yet somehow well-placed) kicks, punches, and head-butts.

He'd already knocked down a good ten soldiers, and the other ten weren't doing much better.

"It's so exciting!" the prince said. "I hope somebody is taking notes! Why didn't I bring any of my scribes? I should send for some!" Rikers stood a short distance from the center of the fight.

Please punch him, I thought, standing up on shaky knees. *Just a little bit.*

But it wasn't to be — Folsom was focused on the soldiers. Himalaya was calling for the soldiers to try to get their hands over Folsom's ears. Where was Bastille? She should have come running at the sounds of the fight.

"The Alcatraz Smedry Theme" continued to play its peppy little melody, coming from somewhere near the prince. "Prince Rikers!" I yelled. "The book! Where is it? We have to close it!"

"Oh, what?" He turned. "Um, I think I dropped it when the fight started."

He was standing near a pile of unsorted books. I cursed, scrambling toward the pile. If we could stop the music, Folsom would stop dancing.

At that moment the battle shifted in my direction. Folsom — his eyes wide with worry and displaying a distinct lack of control — spun through a group of soldiers, throwing four of them into the air.

I stood facing him. I didn't *think* he'd do me any serious harm. I mean, Smedry Talents are unpredictable, but they rarely hurt people too badly.

Except . . . hadn't I used my own Talent to break some arms and cause monsters to topple to their deaths?

Crud, I thought. Folsom raised his fist and prepared to punch directly at my face.

And my Talent engaged.

One of the odd things about Smedry Talents, mine in particular, is how they sometimes act proactively. Mine breaks weapons at a distance if someone tries to kill me.

In this case, something dark and wild seemed to rip from me. I couldn't see it, but I could feel it snapping toward Folsom. His eyes opened wide, and he tripped, his graceful martial-arts power failing him for a brief moment. It was as if he'd suddenly *lost* his Talent.

He toppled to the ground before me. At that moment, a book in the pile beside me exploded, throwing up scraps of paper and glass. The music stopped.

Folsom groaned. The trip left him kneeling right in front of me, confettilike scraps of paper falling around us.

The beast within me quieted, pulling back inside, and all fell still.

When I'd been young, I'd thought of my Talent as a curse. Now I'd begun thinking of it as a kind of wild super-power. This was the first time, however, that I thought of it as something foreign inside of me.

Something alive.

"That was incredible!" said one of the soldiers. I looked up and saw the soldiers regarding me with awe. Himalaya seemed stunned. The prince stood with his arms folded, smiling in contentment at finally getting to witness a battle.

"I saw it," one of the soldiers whispered, "like a wave of power, pulsing out of you, Lord Smedry. It stopped even another Talent."

It felt *good* to be admired. It made me feel like a leader. Like a hero. "See to your friends," I said, pointing to the fallen soldiers. "Give me a report on the wounded." I reached down, helping Folsom to his feet.

He looked down in shame, as Himalaya walked over to comfort him. "Well, I give myself nine out of ten points for being an idiot," he said. "I can't believe I let that happen. I should be able to *control* it!"

"I know how hard it is," I said. "Trust me. It wasn't your fault."

Prince Rikers walked over to join us, his blue robes swishing. "That was wonderful," he said. "Though it's kind of sad how the book turned out."

"I'm heartbroken," I said flatly, glancing about for Bastille. Where *was* she?

"Oh, it's all right," Rikers said, reaching into his pocket. "They have the sequel here too!" He pulled out a book and moved to open the cover.

"Don't you *dare!*" I snapped, grabbing his arm.

"Oh," he said. "Yeah, probably a bad idea." He glanced at my grip on his arm. "You know, you remind me a lot of my sister. I thought you'd be a little less uptight."

"I'm not uptight," I snapped. "I'm annoyed. There's a difference. Himalaya, how's the sorting going?"

"Uh, maybe halfway done," she said. Indeed, the mountains of books were quickly becoming large stacks, like walls. A much smaller stack was particularly interesting to me — it contained books in the Forgotten Language.

There were only four so far, but it was amazing to me that we'd even managed to find them among all the other books. I walked over to the stack, fishing in my jacket pocket for my pair of Translator's Lenses.

I swapped them for my Oculator's Lenses. I almost forgot that I was wearing those. They were starting to feel natural to me, I guess. With the Translator's Lenses on, I could read the titles of the books.

One appeared to be some kind of philosophical work on the nature of laws and justice. Interesting, but I couldn't see it being important enough for my mother to risk so much in order to get.

The other three books were unimpressive. A manual on building chariots, a ledger talking about the number of chickens a particular merchant traded in Athens, and a cookbook. (Hey, I guess even ancient, all-powerful lost societies needed help baking cookies.)

I checked with the soldiers and was relieved to find that none of them was seriously wounded. Folsom had knocked out no fewer than six of them, and some others had broken several limbs. The wounded left for the infirmary and the others returned to helping Himalaya. None of them had seen Bastille.

I wandered through what was quickly becoming a maze of enormous book stacks. Maybe Bastille was looking for signs of the diggers breaking into the room. The scraping sounds had been coming from the southeast corner, but when I neared, I couldn't hear them anymore. Had my mother realized we were on to her? With that sound gone, I could hear something else.

Whispering.

Curious, and a little creeped out, I walked in the direction of the sound. I turned a corner around a wall-like stack of books, and found a little dead-end hollow in the maze.

Bastille lay there, curled up on the cold glass floor, whispering to herself and shivering. I cursed, rushing over to kneel beside her. "Bastille?"

She curled up a little bit further. Her Warrior's Lenses were off, clutched in her hand. I could see a haunted cast to her eyes. A sense of loss, of sorrow, of having had something deep and tender ripped from her, never to be returned.

I felt powerless. Had she been hurt? She shivered and moved, then looked up at me, eyes focusing. She seemed to realize for the first time that I was there.

She immediately pushed away from me and sat up. Then she sighed and wrapped her arms around her knees, bowing her head between them. "Why is it that you always see me like this?" she asked quietly. "I'm strong, I really am."

"I know you are," I said, feeling awkward and embarrassed.

We remained like that for a time, Bastille unresponsive, me feeling like a complete idiot, even though I wasn't sure what I'd done wrong. (Note to all the young men reading this: Get used to that.)

"So . . ." I said. "Er . . . you're still having trouble with that severing thing?"

She looked up, eyes red like they'd been scratched with sandpaper. "It's like . . ." she said in a quiet voice. "It's like I used to have memories. Fond ones, of places I loved, of people I knew. Only now they're gone. I can *feel* the place where they were, and it's a hole, ripped open inside of me."

"The Mindstone is that important?" I asked. It was a dumb thing to say, but I felt I should say *something*.

"It connects all of the Knights of Crystallia," she whispered. "It strengthens us, gives us comfort. By it, we all share a measure of who we are."

"I should have shattered the swords of those idiots who did this to you," I growled.

Bastille shivered, holding her arms close. "I'll get reconnected eventually, so I should probably tell you not to be so angry. They're good people and don't deserve your scorn. But honestly, I'm having trouble feeling sympathy for them right now." She smiled wanly.

I tried to smile back, but it was hard. "Someone *wanted* this to happen to you, Bastille. They set you up."

"Maybe," Bastille said, sighing. It appeared that her episode was over, though it had left her weakened even further.

"Maybe?" I repeated.

"I don't know, Smedry," she said. "Maybe nobody set me up. Maybe I really did just get promoted too quickly, and really did just fail on my own. Maybe . . . maybe there is no grand conspiracy against me."

"I guess you could be right," I said.

You, of course, don't believe that. I mean, when is there *not* some grand conspiracy? This entire series is about a *secret cult of evil Librarians who rule the world*, for Sands' sake.

"Alcatraz?" a voice called. Sing wandered around the corner a moment later. "Himalaya found another book in the Forgotten Language. Figured you would want to look at it."

I glanced at Bastille; she waved me away. "What, you think I need to be babied?" she snapped. "Go. I'll be there in a moment."

I hesitated, but followed Sing around a few walls of books to the center of the room. The prince sat, looking bored, on what appeared to be a throne made of books. (I'm still not sure who he got to make it for him.) Folsom was directing the moving of stacks; Himalaya was still sorting, with no sign of slowing down.

Sing handed me the book. Like all of the others in the Forgotten Language, the text on it looked like crazy scribbles. Before he had died, Alcatraz the First — my ultimate ancestor — had used the Talent to break the language of his people so that nobody could read it.

Nobody, except for someone with a pair of Translator's Lenses. I put mine on and flipped to the first page, hoping it wasn't another cookbook.

Observations on the Talents of the Smedry people, the title page read, *and an explanation of what led up to their fall. As written by Fenilious K. Wandersnag, scribe to His Majesty, Alcatraz Smedry.*

I blinked, then read the words again.

"Guys?" I said, turning. "Guys!"

The group of soldiers hesitated, and Himalaya glanced toward me. I held the book up.

"I think we just found what we've been looking for."

CHAPTER 17

Things are about to go very wrong.

Oh, didn't you know that already? I should think that it would be obvious. We're almost to the end of the book, and we just had a very encouraging victory. Everything looks good. So, of course, it's all going to go wrong. You should pay better attention to plot archetypes.

I'd like to promise you that everything will turn out all right, but I think there's something you should understand. This is the middle book of the series. And, as everyone knows, the heroes *always* lose in the middle book. It makes the series more tense.

Sorry. But hey, at least my books have awesome endings, right?

I dismissed the soldiers, ordering them to return to their posts. Sing and Folsom joined me, looking at the book, even though they couldn't read it. I suspected that my mother must have an Oculator with her to read the book — to her alone, the Lenses would be useless.

"You're sure this is what we're after?" Sing asked, turning the book over in his fingers.

"It's a history of the fall of Incarna," I said, "told by Alcatraz the First's personal scribe."

Sing whistled. "Wow. What are the chances?"

"Pretty good, I'd say," Bastille said, rounding the corner and joining us. She still looked quite the worse for wear, but at least she was standing. I gave her what I hoped was an encouraging smile.

"Nice leer," she said to me. "Anyway, this is the Royal Archives —"

"*Not* a —" Folsom began to say.

"— don't interrupt," Bastille snapped. She appeared to be in rare form — but then, having a piece of your soul cut out tends to do that to people.

"This is the Royal Archives," Bastille continued. "A lot of these books have passed down through the royal Nalhallan line for centuries — and the collection has been added to by the Smedrys, the Knights of Crystallia, and the other noble lines who have joined with us."

"Yes indeed," Prince Rikers said, taking the book from

Sing, looking it over. "People don't just throw away books in the Forgotten Language. A lot of these have been archived here for years and years. They're copies of copies."

"You can copy these scribbles?" I asked with surprise.

"Scribes can be quite meticulous," Sing said. "They're almost as bad as Librarians."

"Excuse me?" Himalaya huffed, walking up to us. She'd finished giving orders to the last couple of soldiers, who were arranging the books she'd just organized. The room looked kind of strange, with the back half of it still dominated by gargantuan piles of books, the front half filled with neatly organized stacks.

"Oh," Sing said. "Um, I didn't mean *you*, Himalaya. I meant Librarians who aren't recovering."

"I'm not either," she said, folding her arms, adopting a very deliberate stance as she stood in her Hushlander skirt and blouse. "I meant what I said earlier. I intend to prove that you can be a Librarian without being evil. There *has* to be a way."

"If you say so . . ." Sing said.

I still kind of agreed with Sing. Librarians were . . . well, Librarians. They'd oppressed me since my childhood. They were trying to conquer Mokia.

"I think you did wonderfully," Folsom said to Himalaya. "Ten out of ten on a scale of pure, majestic effectiveness."

Prince Rikers sniffed at that. "Excuse me," he said, then handed me the Forgotten Language book and walked away.

"What was that about?" Himalaya asked.

"I think Folsom just reminded the prince that he was a book critic," Bastille said.

Folsom sighed. "I don't want to make people mad. I just . . . well, how can people get better if you don't tell them what you honestly think?"

"I don't think everyone wants to hear what you honestly think, Folsom," Himalaya said, laying a hand on his arm.

"Maybe I could go talk to him," Folsom said. "You know, explain myself."

I didn't think the prince would listen, but I didn't say anything as Folsom walked after Rikers. Himalaya was watching after the determined critic with fondness.

"You're in love with him, aren't you?" I asked her.

Himalaya turned, blushing. Bastille immediately punched me in the arm.

"Ow!" I said. (My Talent never seemed to work when Bastille is doing the punching. Perhaps it thought I deserved the punishment.) "Why'd you do that?"

Bastille rolled her eyes. "You don't need to be so blunt, Smedry."

"You're blunt all the time!" I complained. "Why's it wrong when I do it?"

"Because you're *bad* at it, that's why. Now apologize for embarrassing the young woman."

"It's all right," Himalaya said, still blushing. "But, please, don't say such a thing. Folsom is just being kind to me because he knows I feel so lost in Free Kingdoms society. I don't want to burden him with my silliness."

"But, he said — gak!"

"He said 'Gak'?" Himalaya asked, confused. She obviously hadn't seen Bastille step forcefully on my toe in the middle of my sentence.

"Excuse us," Bastille said, smiling at Himalaya, then towing me away. Once we were at a safe distance, she pointed at my face and said, "Don't get involved."

"Why?" I demanded.

"Because they'll work it out on their own, and they don't need you messing things up."

"But I talked to Folsom and he likes her too! I should tell her about it so they can stop acting like lovesick crocodiles."

"Crocodiles?"

"What?" I said defensively. "Crocodiles fall in love. Baby crocodiles come from *somewhere*. Anyway, that's beside the point. We should talk to those two and settle this misunderstanding so they can get on with things."

Bastille rolled her eyes. "How can you be so clever sometimes, Smedry, but such an *idiot* other times?"

"That's unfair, and you —" I stopped. "Wait, you think I'm clever?"

"I said you're clever *sometimes*," she snapped. "Unfortunately, you're annoying *all the time*. If you mess this up, I'll...I don't know. I'll cut off your thumbs and send them to the crocodiles as a wedding present."

I crinkled my brow. "Wait. What?"

She just stalked away. I watched her go, smiling.

She thought I was clever.

I stood in a happy stupor for a few minutes. Finally, I wandered back over to Sing and Himalaya.

"...think about it," Himalaya was saying. "It's not the *Librarian* part that's a problem, it's the *evil* part. I could start a self-help program. World-dominating Cultists Anonymous or something like that."

"I dunno," Sing said, rubbing his chin. "Sounds like you have an uphill battle."

"You Free Kingdomers need to be educated about this as much as the Librarians do!" She smiled at me as I arrived. "Anyway, I feel that we should organize the rest of these books. You know, for consistency's sake."

I looked down at the book in my hands. "Do what you want," I said. "I intend to take this someplace safe. We've probably wasted too much time as it is."

"But what if there are other books in here that are important?" Himalaya asked. "Maybe that's *not* the one your mother wants."

"It is," I said. Somehow I *knew*.

"But how would she even know it was in here?" Himalaya asked. "We didn't."

"My mother's resourceful," I said. "I'll bet she —"

At that moment, Sing tripped.

"Oh, dear!" Himalaya said. "Are you all right — gak!"

She said this last part as I grabbed her by the arm and dived for cover behind a stack of books. To the side, I could see Bastille doing the same with the prince and Folsom. Sing himself rolled over to my hiding place, then got to his knees, looking nervous.

"What are you all *doing*?" Himalaya asked.

I put a finger to my lips, waiting tensely. Sing's Talent, like all of them, couldn't be trusted implicitly — however, he had a good track record of tripping right before dangerous events. His foresight — or, well, his clumsiness — had saved my life back in the Hushlands.

I almost thought that this one was a false alarm. And then I heard it. Voices.

The door to the room opened, and my mother walked in.

Oh, wait. You're still here? I thought that last line was going to end the chapter. It seemed like a nice, dramatic place.

Chapter isn't long enough yet? Really? Hum. Well, guess we'll move on, then. Ahem.

I stared in shock. That really *was* my mother, Shasta Smedry. She'd ditched the wig she'd been wearing at the party and wore her usual blond hair up in a bun, along with standard-issue horn-rimmed glasses. Her face was so hard.

Emotionless. Even more so than what I'd seen from other Librarians.

My heart twisted. Other than the faint glimpses of her I'd caught earlier in the day, this was the first time I'd seen her since the library in my hometown. The first time I'd seen her since . . . learning that she was my mother.

Shasta was accompanied by a dangerously large group of Librarian thugs — oversized, muscle-bound types that wore bow ties and glasses. (Kind of like a genetic mutant created by mixing nerd DNA with linebacker DNA. I'll bet they spend their free time giving themselves wedgies, then stuffing themselves in lockers.)

Also with her was a young, freckled man about twenty years old. He wore a sweater-vest and slacks (Librarian-type clothing) and had on glasses. Tinted ones.

A Dark Oculator, I thought. *So I was right.* He would be there to use the Translator's Lenses for her, but this guy didn't seem *nearly* as dangerous as Blackburn had been. Of course, my mother more than made up for the difference.

But how had they gotten by the soldiers on the stairs? It looked like Sing had been right, and they'd been tunneling into the stairwell. Shouldn't we have heard sounds of fighting? What of the two knights on duty? I itched to rush out and see what had happened.

The group of Librarians stopped at the front of the room. I remained hidden behind my wall of books. Bastille had successfully pulled the prince and Folsom behind another wall of books, and I could just barely see her peeking around the corner. She and I met each other's eyes, and I could see the questions in her face.

Something very odd was going on. Why hadn't we heard any sounds of fighting from the stairwell?

"Something very odd is going on here," my mother said, her voice echoing in the quiet room. "Why are all of these books stacked like this?"

The freckled Oculator adjusted his spectacles. Fortunately, they weren't red-tinted Oculator's Lenses — which would have let him notice me — but were instead tinted with orange-and-blue stripes. I didn't recognize that type.

"The scholars I interviewed said the place was messy, Shasta," he said in a kind of nasal voice, "but who knows what they consider clean or messy? These stacks look like they were arranged and organized by a buffoon!"

Himalaya huffed in outrage, and Sing had to grab her by the arm to keep her from marching out to defend her cataloging abilities.

"All right," Shasta said. "I don't know how long it will be before someone notices what we've done. I want to find that book and get out of here as soon as possible."

I frowned. That made it seem like they had gotten into the room by stealth. It was a good plan; if a book disappeared from the Royal-Archives-Not-a-Library™, then it would probably be centuries before anyone realized it was gone. If they even realized it at all.

But that meant my mother and a group of about thirty Librarians had managed to *sneak* past the archives' defenses. That seemed impossible.

Either way, we were in trouble. I didn't have any offensive Lenses, and Bastille's severing had her on the brink of collapse. That left us with Folsom. I'd just seen him do some serious damage, but I hated trusting a Smedry Talent as unpredictable as his.

It seemed a far, far better idea to get out and grab our army, then come back for a fight. I liked that idea a whole lot, particularly since we'd probably be able to send to the palace for Grandpa Smedry. (And maybe the Free Kingdomer version of a Sherman tank or two.)

But how to get out? The Librarians were beginning to move through the stacks. We were near the middle of the room, our position shadowed by a lack of lamplight, but we obviously couldn't remain hidden for long.

"All right," I whispered to Sing and Himalaya, "we need to get out of here! Any ideas?"

"Maybe we could sneak around the outside of the room," Himalaya said, pointing at the mazelike corridors.

I didn't like the idea of risking running into one of those thugs. I shook my head.

"We could hide in the back," Sing whispered. "Hope they get frustrated and leave. . . ."

"Sing, this is a whole *group* of Librarians," I said. "They'll all be able to do what Himalaya did. They'll sort through this room in minutes!"

Himalaya snorted quietly. "I doubt it," she said. "I was one of the Wardens of the Standard — the best sorters in all the world. Most of those are just basic acolytes. They'll barely be able to alphabetize, let alone sort based on the Sticky Hamstring methodology."

"Either way," I whispered, "I doubt they're going to leave without *this*." I glanced down at the volume I still carried, then looked across the central aisle to Bastille. She looked tense, poised. She was getting ready to fight — which tended to be her solution to a lot of things.

Great, I thought. *This is* not *going to end well.*

"If only my sister were here," Sing said. "She could make herself look like one of those thugs and slip away."

I froze. Sing's sister, Australia, would be back with the Mokian contingent trying to lobby the Council of Kings to make the right decision. She had the Talent to go to sleep, then wake up looking really ugly. That usually meant looking like someone else for a short time. We didn't have her, but we did have the Disguiser's Lenses. I hurriedly pulled them out. They could get me out — but what about the others?

I looked across the corridor. Bastille met my eyes, then saw the Lenses in my hands. I could tell she recognized them. She met my eyes, then nodded.

Go, the look said. *Take that book to safety. Don't worry about us.*

If you've read through my series this far, then you know that at that age I considered myself too noble to abandon my friends. I was starting to change, however. My nibble of fame — one I still secretly longed to taste again — had begun to work inside me.

I put on the Lenses and focused, imagining the image of a Librarian thug. Himalaya gasped quietly as I changed, and Sing raised an eyebrow. I glanced at them.

"Be ready to run," I said. I looked at Bastille and held up one finger to indicate that she should wait. Then I pointed at the door. She seemed to get my meaning.

I took a deep breath, then stepped out. The center of the room was poorly lit, since we'd obscured a lot of the lamps with book walls. Those lamps were hung back in their places on the walls, even the one I'd tried to use to burn the place down.

I walked forward, holding my breath, expecting the Librarians to raise an alarm against me, but they were too busy searching. Nobody even turned. I walked right up to my mother. She glanced at me, the woman I'd always known as Ms. Fletcher, the woman who had spent years berating me as a child.

"Well, what is it?" she snapped, and I realized I'd just been standing there, staring.

I held up the book, the one she was searching for. Her eyes opened wide with anticipation.

And so, I handed the book to her.

Is this a good place? Can I stop here now? Okay, finally. About time.

CHAPTER 18

I'd like to apologize. Way back in my first book of this series, near the end, I made fun of the fact that readers sometimes stay up *way* too late reading books. I know how it is. You get involved in a story and you don't want to stop. Then the author does very unfair things, like confront his mother face-to-face at the end of the chapter, forcing you to turn to the next page and read what happens next.

This sort of thing is terribly unfair, and I shouldn't be engaging in such activities. After all, there is one thing that every good book should have in it: That, of course, is a potty break.

Sure, we characters can go between chapters, but what about you? You have to wait until there's a portion of the book that is slow and boring. And since those don't *exist* in my books, I force you to wait until the story is done. That's just not fair. And so, get ready, here's your chance. It's time for the slow, boring part.

The furry panda is a noble creature, known for its excellent chess-playing skills. Pandas often play chess in exchange for lederhosen, which make up a large chunk of their preferred diet. They also make a fortune off their licensing deals, in which they shrink and stuff members of their clan and sell them as plush toys for young children. It is often theorized that one day, all of these plush pandas will decide to rise up and rule the world. And that will be fun, because pandas rock.

Okay, done doing your business? Great. Now maybe we can finally get on with this story. (It's really annoying to have to wait for you like that, so you should thank me for my patience.)

My mother took the book from me and waved eagerly to the freckled Dark Oculator. "Fitzroy, get over here."

"Yes, yes, Shasta," he said a little too eagerly. He regarded her adoringly. "What is it?"

"Read this," she said, handing him the book and the Translator's Lenses.

The young man grabbed the book and the Lenses; it

disgusted me how eager he was to please my mother. I inched away, raising my hand toward the nearby wall.

"Hum, yes . . ." Fitzroy said. "Shasta, this is it! The very book we wanted!"

"Excellent," my mother said, reaching for the book.

At that moment, I touched the glass wall and released a powerful blast of breaking power into it. Now, I knew I couldn't break the glass — I was counting on that. In previous circumstances, I'd been able to use things like walls, tables, even smoke trails as a conduit. Like a wire carried electricity, an object could carry my breaking power within it, shattering something on the other end.

It was a risk, but I wasn't going to leave my allies alone in a room full of Librarians. Particularly not when one of those allies was the official Alcatraz Smedry novelist. I had my legacy to think about.

Fortunately, it worked. The breaking power moved through the wall like ripples on a lake. The lamps on the walls shattered.

And everything plunged into darkness.

I leaped forward and snatched the book, which was being passed between Shasta and Fitzroy. Voices called out in shock and surprise, and I distinctly heard my mother curse. I rushed for the doorway, bursting out into the lit hallway beyond and quickly taking off my Disguiser's lenses.

There was a sudden crash from inside the room. Then a face appeared from the darkness. It was a Librarian thug. I cringed, preparing for a fight, but the man suddenly grimaced in pain and fell to the ground. Bastille jumped over him as he groaned and grabbed his leg; her brother, the prince, ran along behind her.

I ushered Rikers through the door, relieved that Bastille had understood my hand gestures. (Though I used the universal signal for "Wait here for a sec, then run for the door," that signal also happens to be the universal hand sign for "I need a milk shake; I think I'll find one in that direction.")

"Where's Folsom —" I began, but the critic soon appeared, carrying Rikers's novel in his hand, prepared to open the cover and start dancing at a moment's notice. He puffed, coming through the door as Bastille knocked aside another thug who was clever enough to make for the light. Only a few seconds had passed, but I began to worry. Where were Sing and Himalaya?

"I give this escape a three and a half out of seven and

six-eighths, Alcatraz," Folsom said nervously. "Clever in concept, but rather nerve-wracking in execution."

"Noted," I said tensely, glancing about. Where *were* those soldiers of ours? They were supposed to be out in the stairwell here, but it was empty. In fact, something seemed odd about the stairwell.

"Guys?" Rikers said. "I think —"

"There!" Bastille said, pointing as Sing and Himalaya appeared from the shadows of the room. The two rushed through the door, and I slammed it closed, using my breaking power to jam the lock. "What was that crash?" I asked.

"I tripped into a couple rows of books," Sing said, "throwing them down on the Librarians to keep them distracted."

"Smart," I said. "Let's get out of here."

We began to rush up the stairwell, the wooden steps creaking beneath our feet. "That was risky, Smedry," Bastille said.

"You expected less of me?"

"Of course not," she snapped. "But why hand the book over to the Librarian?"

"I got it back," I said, holding it up. "Plus, now we know for sure that *this* is the volume they wanted."

Bastille cocked her head. "Huh. You *are* clever some-times."

I smiled. Unfortunately, the truth is, *none* of us was being very clever at that moment. None of us but Rikers, of course — and we'd chosen to ignore him. That's usually a safe move.

Except, of course, when you're rushing up the wrong stairwell. It finally dawned on me, and I froze in place, causing the others to stumble to a halt.

"What is it, Alcatraz?" Sing asked.

"The stairs," I said. "They're wooden."

"So?"

"They were stone before."

"That's what I've been trying to say!" Prince Rikers exclaimed. "I wonder how they turned the steps to a different material."

I suddenly felt a sense of horror. The door was just above us. I walked up nervously and pushed on it.

It opened into a medieval-looking castle chamber completely different from the one that had held our soldiers. This room had red carpeting, library stacks in the distance, and was filled with a good *two hundred* Librarian soldiers.

"Shattering Glass!" Bastille cursed, slamming the door in front of me. "What's going on?"

I ignored her for the moment, rushing back down the steps. The Librarians locked inside the archives room were pounding on the door, trying to break it down. Now that I paused to consider, the landing right in front of the door looked very different from the way it had before. It was far larger, and it had a door at the left side.

As the others piled down the steps after me, I threw open the door to my left. I stepped into an enormous chamber filled with wires, panes of glass, and scientists in white lab coats. There were large containers on the sides of the room. Containers that I'm sure were filled with brightsand.

"What in the *Sands* is going on?" Folsom demanded, peeking in behind me.

I stood, stunned. "We're not in the same building anymore, Folsom."

"What?"

"They swapped us! The archive filled with books — the *entire glass room* — they swapped it for another room using Transporter's Glass! They weren't digging a tunnel to get in, they were digging to the corners so they could affix glass there and teleport the room away!"

It was brilliant. The glass was unbreakable, the stairwell guarded. But what if you could take the whole room away and replace it with another one? You could search out the book you needed, then swap the rooms back, and nobody would be the wiser.

The door behind us broke open, and I turned to see a group of muscular Librarians force their way into the stairwell. I could just barely make out Bastille tensing for combat, and Folsom moved to open the novel with the music.

"No," I said to them. "We're beaten. Don't waste your energy fighting."

Part of me found it strange that they listened to me. Even Bastille obeyed my command. I would have expected the prince to preempt me and take charge, but he seemed perfectly content to stand and watch. He even seemed excited.

"Wonderful!" he whispered to me. "We've been captured!"

Great, I thought as my mother pushed her way out through the broken door. She saw me and smiled — a rare expression for her. It was the smile of a cat who'd just found a mouse to play with.

"Alcatraz," she said.

"Mother," I replied coldly.

She raised an eyebrow. "Tie them up," she said to her thugs. "And fetch that book for me."

The thugs pulled out swords and herded us into the room with the scientists.

"Why'd you stop me?" Bastille hissed.

"Because it wouldn't have done any good," I whispered back. "We don't even know where we are — we could be back in the Hushlands, for all we know. We have to get back to the Royal Archives."

I waited for it, but nobody said the inevitable "not a library." I realized that nobody else could hear us — which, indeed, is kind of the point of whispering in the first place. (That, and sounding more mysterious.)

"How do we get back, then?" Bastille asked.

I glanced at the equipment around us. We had to activate the silimatic machines and swap the rooms again. But how?

Before I could ask Bastille about this, the thugs pulled us all apart and bound us with ropes. This wasn't too big a deal — my Talent could snap ropes in a heartbeat, and if the thugs assumed that we were tied up, then maybe they'd get lax and give us a better chance for escaping.

The Librarians began to rifle through our pockets, depositing our possessions — including all of my Lenses — on a low table. Then they forced us to the ground, which was sterile and white. The room itself bustled with activity as Librarians and scientists checked monitors, wires, and panes of glass.

My mother flipped through the book on Smedry history, though — of course — she couldn't read it. Her lackey, Fitzroy, was more interested in my Lenses. "The other pair of Translator's Lenses," he said, picking them up. "These will be very nice to have."

He slid them into his pocket, continuing on to the others. "Oculator's Lenses," he said, "boring." He set those aside. "A single, untinted Lens," he said, looking over the Truthfinder's Lens. "It's probably worthless." He handed the Lens to a scientist, who snapped it into a spectacle frame.

"Ah!" Fitzroy continued. "Are those Disguiser's Lenses? Now *these* are valuable!"

The scientist returned the spectacles with the single Truthfinder's Lens in them, but Fitzroy set this aside, picking up the violet Disguiser's Lenses and putting them on. He immediately shifted shapes, melding to look like a much more muscular and handsome version of himself. "Hum, very nice," he said, inspecting his arms.

Why didn't I think of that? I thought.

"Oh, I almost forgot," Shasta said, pulling something out of her purse. She tossed a few glass rings to her Librarian thugs. "Put those on that one, that one, and that one." She pointed at me, Folsom, and Sing.

The three Smedrys. That seemed ominous. Perhaps it was time to try an escape. But . . . we were surrounded and we still didn't know how to use the machines to get us back. Before I could make up my mind, one of the thugs snapped a ring on my arm and locked it.

I didn't feel any different.

"What you aren't feeling," my mother said offhandedly, "is the loss of your Talent. That's Inhibitor's Glass."

"Inhibitor's Glass is a myth!" Sing said, aghast.

"Not according to the Incarna people," my mother said, smiling. "You'd be amazed what we're learning from these Forgotten Language books." She snapped the book in her hands closed. I could see a smug satisfaction in her smile as she pulled open a drawer beneath the table and dropped the book in it. She closed the drawer, then — oddly — she picked up one of the rings of Inhibitor's Glass and snapped it onto her own arm.

"Handy things, these rings," she said. "Smedry Talents are far more useful when you can determine exactly when they are to activate." My mother had my father's same Talent — losing things — which she'd gained by marriage. My grandfather said he thought she'd never learned to control it, so I could guess why she'd want to wear Inhibitor's Glass.

"You people," Sing said, struggling as the thugs snapped a ring on his arm. "All you want to do is control. You want everything to be normal and boring, no freedom or uncertainty."

"I couldn't have said it better myself," my mother said, putting her hands behind her back.

This was getting bad. I cursed myself. I should have let Bastille fight, then tried to find a way to activate the swap during the confusion. Without our Talents, we were in serious trouble. I tested my Talent anyway, but got nothing. It was a very odd feeling. Like trying to start your car, but only getting a pitiful grinding sound.

I wiggled my arm, trying to see if I could get the ring of Inhibitor's Glass off, but it was on tight. I ground my teeth. Maybe I could use the Lenses on the table somehow.

Unfortunately, the only Lenses left were my basic Oculator's Lenses and the single Truthfinder's Lens. *Great*, I thought, wishing — not for the first time — that Grandpa Smedry had given me some Lenses that I could use in a fight.

Still, I had to work with what I had. I stretched my neck, wiggling to the side, and finally managed to touch the side of the Truthfinder's spectacles with my cheek. I could activate them as long as I was touching the frames.

"You are a monster," Sing said, still talking to my mother.

"A monster?" Shasta asked. "Because I like order? I think you'll agree with our way, once you see what we can do for the Free Kingdoms. Aren't you Sing Sing Smedry the anthropologist? I hear that you're fascinated by the Hushlands. Why speak such harsh words about Librarians if you are so fascinated by our lands?"

Sing fell silent.

"Yes," Shasta said. "Everything will be better when the Librarians rule."

I froze. I could just barely see her through the side of the Lens by my head on the table. And those words she'd just spoken — they weren't completely true. When she'd said them, to my eyes she'd released a patch of air that was muddied and gray. It was as if my mother herself weren't sure that she was telling the truth.

"Lady Fletcher," one of the Librarian thugs said, approaching. "I have informed my superiors of our captives."

Shasta frowned. "I . . . see."

"You will, of course, deliver them to us," the Librarian soldier said. "I believe that is Prince Rikers Dartmoor — he could prove to be a very valuable captive."

"These are *my* captives, Captain," Shasta said. "I'll decide what to do with them."

"Oh? This equipment and these scientists belong to the Scrivener's Bones. All you were promised was the book. You said we could have anything else in the room we wanted. Well, these people are what we demand."

Scrivener's Bones, I thought. *That explains all the wires.* The Scrivener's Bones were the Librarian sect who liked to mix Free Kingdoms technology and Hushlander technology. That was probably why there were wires leading from the brightsand containers. Rather than just opening the containers and bathing the glass in light, the Librarians used wires and switches.

That could be a big help. It meant there might be a way to use the machinery to activate the swap.

"We are very insistent," the leader of the Librarian soldiers said. "You can have the book and the Lenses. We will take the captives."

"Very well," my mother snapped. "You can have them. But I want half of my payment back as compensation."

I felt a stab inside my chest. So she *would* sell me. As if I were nothing.

"But, Shasta," the young Librarian Oculator said, stepping up to her. "You'll give them up? Even the boy?"

"He means nothing to me."

I froze.

It was a lie.

I could see it plain and clear through the corner of the Lens. When she spoke the words, black sludge fell from her lips.

"Shasta Smedry," the soldier said, smiling. "The woman

who would marry just to get a Talent, and who would spawn a child just to sell him to the highest bidder!"

"Why should I feel anything for the son of a Nalhallan? Take the boy. I don't care."

Another lie.

"Let's just get on with this," she finished. Her manner was so controlled, so calm. You'd never have known that she was lying through her teeth.

But . . . what did it *mean*? She couldn't care for me. She was a terrible, vile person. Monsters like her didn't have feelings.

She *couldn't* care about me. I didn't want her to. It was so much more simple to assume that she was heartless.

"What about Father?" I found myself whispering. "Do you hate him too?"

She turned toward me, meeting my eyes. She parted her lips to speak, and I thought I caught a trail of black smoke begin to slip out and pour toward the ground.

Then it stopped. "What's he doing?" she snapped, pointing. "Fitzroy, I thought I told you to keep those Lenses secured!"

The Oculator jumped in shock, rushing over and grabbing the Truthfinder's Lens and pocketing it. "Sorry," he said. He took the other Lenses and placed them in another pocket of his coat.

I leaned back, feeling frustrated. What now?

I was the brave and brilliant Alcatraz Smedry. Books had been written about me. Rikers was smiling, as if this were all a big adventure. And I could guess why. He didn't feel threatened. He had me to save him.

It was then that I understood what Grandpa Smedry had been trying to tell me. Fame itself wasn't a bad thing. Praise wasn't a bad thing. The danger was assuming that you really *were* what everyone imagined you to be.

I'd come into this all presuming that my Talent could get us out. Well, now it *couldn't*. I'd brought us into danger because I'd let my self-confidence make me overconfident.

And you all are to blame for this, in part. This is what your adoration does. You create for yourselves heroes using our names, but those fabrications are so incredible, so elevated that the real thing can never live up to them. You destroy us, consume us.

And I am what's left over when you're done.

CHAPTER 19

Oh, wasn't that how you expected me to end that last chapter? Was it kind of a downer? Made you feel bad about yourself?

Well, good.

We're getting near the end, and I'm tired of putting on a show for you. I've tried to prove that I'm arrogant and selfish, but I just don't think you're buying it. So, maybe if I make the book a depressing pile of slop, you'll leave me alone.

"Alcatraz?" Bastille whispered.

I mean, why is it that you readers always assume that you're never to blame for anything? You just sit there, comfortable on your couch while we suffer. You can *enjoy* our pain and our misery because *you're* safe.

Well, this is real to me. It's real. It still affects me. Ruins me.

"Alcatraz?" Bastille repeated.

I am not a god. I am not a hero. I can't be what you want me to be. I can't save people, or protect them, because I can't even save myself!

I am a murderer. Do you understand? *I KILLED HIM.*

"Alcatraz!" Bastille hissed.

I looked up from my bonds. A good half hour had passed. We were still captive, and I'd tried dozens of times to summon my Talent. It was unresponsive. Like a sleeping beast that refused to awaken. I was powerless.

My mother chatted with the other Librarians, who had sent in teams to rifle through the books and determine if there was anything else of value inside the archives. From what I'd heard when I cared enough to pay attention, they were planning on swapping the rooms back soon.

Sing had tried to crawl away at one point. He had earned himself a boot to the face — he was already beginning to get a black eye. Himalaya sniffled quietly, leaning against Folsom. Prince Rikers continued to sit happily, as if this were all a big exciting amusement-park ride.

"We need to escape," Bastille said. "We need to get out. The treaty will be ratified in a matter of minutes!"

"I've failed, Bastille," I whispered. "I can't get us out."

"Alcatraz . . ." she said. She sounded so exhausted. I glanced at her and saw the haunted fatigue from before, but it seemed even worse.

"I can barely keep myself awake," she whispered. "This hole inside . . . it seems to be chewing on my mind, sucking out everything I think and feel. I can't do this without you. You've *got* to lead us. I love my brother, but he's useless."

"That's the problem," I said, leaning back. "I am too."

The Librarians were approaching. I stiffened, but they didn't come for me. Instead, they grabbed Himalaya.

She cried out, struggling.

"Let go of her!" Folsom bellowed. "What are you doing?"

He tried to jump after them, but his hands and legs were tied, and all he managed to do was lurch forward onto his face. The Librarian thugs smiled, shoving him to the side, where he caused the table beside us to topple over. It scattered our possessions — some keys, a couple of coin pouches, one book — to the floor.

The book was the volume of *Alcatraz Smedry and the Mechanic's Wrench* that Folsom had been carrying earlier, and it fell open to the front page. My theme music began to play, and I tensed, hoping for Folsom to attack.

But, of course, he didn't. He wore the Inhibitor's Glass

on his arm. The little melody continued to sound; it was supposed to be brave and triumphant, but now it seemed a cruel parody.

My theme music played while I failed.

"What are you doing to her?" Folsom repeated, struggling uselessly as a Librarian stood with his boot on Folsom's back.

The young Oculator Fitzroy approached; he still wore my Disguiser's Lenses, which gave him an illusionary body that made him look handsome and strong. "We've had a request," he said. "From She Who Cannot Be Named."

"You're in contact with *her*?" Sing demanded.

"Of course we are," Fitzroy said. "We Librarian sects get along far better than you all would like to think. Now, Ms. Snorgan . . . Sorgavag . . . She Who Cannot Be Named was *not* pleased to discover that Shasta's team had planned to steal the Royal Archives — *definitely* a library — on the very day of the treaty ratification. However, when she heard about a very special captive we'd obtained, she was a little more forgiving."

"You shall never get away with this, foul monster!" Prince Rikers suddenly exclaimed. "You may hurt me, but you shall never wound me!"

We all stared at him.

"How was that?" he asked me. "I think it was a good line. Maybe I should do it over. You know, get more baritone into it. When the villain talks about me, I should respond, right?"

"I wasn't talking about you," Fitzroy said, shaking Himalaya. "I'm talking about She Who Cannot Be Named's former assistant. I think it's time to show you all what happens when someone betrays the Librarians."

I had sudden flashbacks to being tortured by Blackburn. The Dark Oculators seemed to delight in pain and suffering.

It didn't seem that Fitzroy was even going to bother with the torture part. The thugs held Himalaya back, and Fitzroy produced a knife. He held it to her neck. Sing began to cry out, requiring several guards to hold him down. Folsom was bellowing in rage. Librarian scientists just continued monitoring their equipment in the background.

This is what it came down to. Me, too weak to help. I was nothing without my Talent or my Lenses.

"Alcatraz," Bastille whispered. Somehow I heard her over all the other noise. "I believe in you."

It was virtually the same thing others had been telling me since I'd arrived in Nalhalla. But those things had all been lies. They hadn't known me.

But Bastille did. And she believed in me.

From her, that *meant* something.

I turned with desperation, looking at Himalaya, who was held captive, weeping. Fitzroy seemed to be enjoying the pain he was causing the rest of us by holding that knife to her throat. I knew, at that moment, that he really intended to kill her. He would murder her in front of the man who loved her.

Who *loved* her.

My Lenses were gone. My Talent was gone. I only had one thing left.

I was a *Smedry*.

"Folsom!" I screamed. "Do you love her?"

"What?" he asked.

"Do you love Himalaya?"

"Of course I do! Please, don't let him kill her!"

"Himalaya," I demanded, "do you love him?"

She nodded as the knife began to cut. It was enough.

"Then I pronounce you married," I said.

Everyone froze for a moment. A short distance away, my mother turned and looked at us, suddenly alarmed. Fitzroy raised an eyebrow, his knife slightly bloodied. My theme music played faintly from the little book on the floor.

"Well, that's touching," Fitzroy said. "Now you can die as a married woman! I —"

At that moment, Himalaya's fist took him in the face.

The ropes that bound her fell to the ground, snapped and broken, as she leaped into the air and kicked the two thugs beside her. The men went down, unconscious, and Himalaya spun like a dancer toward the group standing behind. She cleared them all with a sweeping kick, delivered precisely, despite the fact that she seemed to have no idea what she was doing.

Her face was determined, her eyes wide with rage; a little trickle of blood ran down her throat. She twisted and spun, fighting with a beautiful, uncoordinated rage, fully under the control of her brand-new Talent.

She was now Himalaya Smedry. And, as everyone knows (and I believe I've pointed out to you), when you marry a Smedry, you get their Talent.

I rolled to where Fitzroy had fallen. More important, where his knife had fallen. I kicked it across the floor to

Bastille, who — being Bastille — caught it even though her hands (literally) were tied behind her back. In a second, she'd cut herself free. In another second, both Sing and I were free.

Fitzroy sat up, holding his cheek, dazed. I grabbed the Disguiser's Lenses off his face, and he immediately shrank back to being spindly and freckled. "Sing, grab him and make for the archives room!"

The hefty Mokian didn't need to hear that again. He easily tucked the squirming Fitzroy under his arm while Bastille attacked the thugs who were holding Folsom down, defeating them both. But then she wavered nauseously.

"Get to the room, everyone!" I yelled as Himalaya kept the thugs at bay. Bastille nodded, wobbling as she helped the prince to his feet. Shasta watched from the side, yelling for the thugs to attack — but they were wary of engaging a Smedry Talent.

After struggling for a second to get that band of glass off my arm — it wouldn't budge — I pulled open the drawer of the table and snatched the book my mother had stowed there.

That left us with one major problem. We were right back where we'd been when I'd made us surrender.

Retreating into the archives room wouldn't help if we remained surrounded by Librarians. We had to activate the swap. Unfortunately, there was no *way* I'd be able to reach those terminals. I figured I only had one chance.

Folsom rushed past, grabbing the still-playing music book off the ground and snapping it closed so Himalaya could come out of her super-kung-fu-Librarian-chick trance. She froze midkick, looking dazed. She had dropped all the thugs around her. Folsom grabbed her by the shoulder and spun her into a kiss. Then he pulled her after the others.

That only left me. I looked across the room at my mother, who met my eyes. She seemed rather self-confident, considering what had happened, and I figured that *she* figured that I couldn't escape. Go figure.

I grabbed the pile of electrical cords off the ground and — pulling as hard as I could — yanked them out of their sockets in the machinery. Then I raced after my friends.

Bastille waited at the door that led into the archives room. "What's that?" she said, pointing at the cords.

"Our only chance," I replied, ducking into the room. She followed, then slammed the door — or, at least, what was left of it. It was pitch dark inside. I'd broken the lamps. I heard the breathing of my little group, shallow, worried.

"What now?" Sing whispered.

I held the cords in my hands. I touched the tips with my fingers, then closed my eyes. This was a big gamble. Sure, I'd been able to make the music box work, but this was something completely different.

I didn't have time to doubt myself. The Librarians would be upon us in a few moments. I held those cords, held my breath, and activated them like I would a pair of Oculator's Lenses.

Immediately, something drained from me. My strength was sapped away, and I felt a shock of exhaustion — as if my body had decided to run a marathon when I wasn't looking. I dropped the cords, wobbling, and reached out to steady myself against Sing.

"You're all dead, you know," Fitzroy sputtered in the darkness; he was still held — I assumed — under Sing's arm. "They'll burst in here in a second and then you're dead. What did you think? You're trapped! Sandless idiots!"

I took a deep breath, righting myself. Then I pushed the door open.

The blond Knight of Crystallia standing guard was still outside. "You all right?" she asked, peeking in. "What happened?" Behind her, I could see the stone stairwell of the Royal Archives, still packed with soldiers.

"We're back!" Sing said. "How . . . ?"

"You powered the glass," Bastille said, looking at me. "Like you did with Rikers's silimatic music box. You initiated a swap!"

I nodded. At my feet, the cords to the Librarian machinery lay cut at the ends. Our swap had severed them where they'd poked through the door.

"Shattering Glass, Smedry!" Bastille said. "How in the name of the first Sands did you do that?"

"I don't know," I said, rushing out the doorway. "We can worry about it later. Right now, we've got to save Mokia."

CHAPTER 20

Questions.

We're at the end, and you probably have a few of them. If you've been paying attention closely, you probably have more than just "a few."

You should probably have more than you do.

I've tried to be honest, as honest as I can be. I haven't lied about anything important.

But some of the people in the story . . . well, they're lying for certain.

No matter how much you think you know, there is always more to learn. It all has to do with Librarians, knights, and, of course, fish sticks. Enjoy this next part. I'll see you in the Epilogue.

"Aha!" I said, pulling not one but *two* pairs of Translator's Lenses from Fitzroy's jacket. The Dark Oculator himself lay tied up on the floor as we rode in the prince's giant glass pig. I'd told my soldiers to get some sort of equipment and dig to the corner of the archives room and remove the glass there, so that the Librarians couldn't swap the room back and steal any of the other books.

"I still don't understand what happened," Sing said, sitting nervously as our vehicle plodded toward the palace.

"Oculators can power glass," I said. "Like Lenses."

"Lenses are magic," Sing said. "That Transporter's Glass was technology."

"The two are more similar than you think, Sing. In fact, I think *all* of these powers are connected. Do you remember what you said when you and I were hiding down there a few moments ago? The thing about your sister?"

"Sure," Sing said. "I mentioned that I wished she'd been there, because she could have imitated one of the Librarians."

"Which I could do with these," I said, holding up the pair of Disguiser's Lenses, which we'd retrieved from Fitzroy. "Sing, these work *just* like Australia's Talent does. If she falls asleep thinking about somebody, she wakes up looking just like them. Well, if I wear these and concentrate, I can do the same thing."

"What are you saying, Alcatraz?" Folsom asked.

"I'm not sure," I admitted. "It just seems suspicious to me. I mean, look at your Talent. It makes you a better warrior when you hear music, right?"

He nodded.

"Well, what do Bastille's Warrior's Lenses do?" I said. "They make her a better fighter. My uncle Kaz's Talent lets him transport people across great distances, which sounds an awful lot like what that Transporter's Glass did."

"Yes," Sing said. "But what about your grandfather's Talent? It lets him arrive late to things, and there aren't Lenses that do *that*."

"There are lots of types of glass we don't know about," I said. I picked up one of the rings of Inhibitor's Glass, which we'd managed to get off our arms using a set of keys in Fitzroy's pocket. "You thought these were mythical."

Sing fell silent, and I turned, watching through the translucent walls as we approached the palace. "I think this is all related," I said more softly. "The Smedry Talents, silimatic technology, Oculators . . . and whatever it is my mother is trying to accomplish. It's all connected."

She didn't believe what she said about the Librarians ruling everything. She wasn't certain.

She has different goals from the other Librarians. But what are they?

I sighed, shaking my head, reaching over to pick up the book we'd brought from the archives. At least we had it, as well as both pairs of Translator's Lenses. I slipped the Lenses on, then glanced at the first page.

Soups for everyone, it read. *A guide to the best Greek and Incarna cooking.*

I froze. I flipped through the book anxiously, then took off the Lenses and tried the other pair. Both showed the same thing.

This wasn't the same book.

"What?" Sing asked. "Alcatraz, what is it?"

"She switched books on us!" I said, frustrated. "This isn't the book on Incarna history — it's the cookbook!" I'd seen her work with deft fingers before, when she'd snatched the Sands of Rashid right out from under my nose back in my room in the Hushlands. Plus, she had access to my father's Talent of losing things. It might be of help in hiding stuff.

I slammed the book back down on the table. Around me, the rich, red-furnished room shook as the glass pig continued on its way.

"That's not important right now," Bastille said in an exhausted voice. She sat on the couch beside Folsom and Himalaya, and she looked like she'd gotten even worse since we'd left the Librarians. Her eyes were unfocused, as if she'd been drugged, and she kept rubbing her temples.

"We need to stop the treaty first," she said. "Your mother can't do anything with that book as long as *you* have both pairs of Translator's Lenses."

She was right. Mokia had to be our focus now. As the pig pulled up to the palace, I took a deep breath. "All right," I said. "You all know what to do?"

Sing, Folsom, Himalaya, and Prince Rikers each nodded. We'd discussed our plan during the chapter break. (Neener, neener.)

"The Librarians aren't likely to let this go smoothly," I said, "but I doubt there will be much they can do with all of the soldiers and knights guarding the palace. However, they're Librarians, so be ready for anything."

They nodded again. We prepared to go, and the door on the pig's butt opened. (I think that undermined our dramatic exit.) Bastille stood to go with us, wobbling on unsteady feet.

"Uh, Bastille," I said. "I think you should wait here."

She gave me a stiff glance — the kind that made me feel like I'd just been smacked across the face with a broom. I took that as her answer.

"All right," I said with a sigh. "Let's go, then."

We marched out of the pig and up the steps. Prince Rikers called for guards immediately — I think he just liked the drama of having a full troop of soldiers with us. Indeed, our entrance into the hallway with the wall-hanging panes of glass was rather intimidating.

The Knights of Crystallia standing at attention in the hallway saluted us as we passed, and I felt significantly more safe, knowing they were there.

"Do you think your mother will have warned the others of what happened?" Sing whispered.

"I doubt it," I said. "Mother's allies contacted She Who Cannot Be Named to gloat over having captured some valuable prisoners. You don't call to gloat over having lost those same prisoners. I think we'll surprise them."

"I hope so," Sing said as we approached the doors to the council room. We nodded to the pair of knights, and then I stepped aside.

"Time for your big entrance, Your Highness," I said, gesturing for Prince Rikers.

"Really?" he said. "I get to do it?"

"Go ahead," I said.

The prince dusted himself off. He smiled broadly, then strode through the doors into the chamber and bellowed in a loud voice, "In the name of all that is just, I demand these proceedings to be halted!"

Down below, the monarchs sat around their table, a large document set out before them. King Dartmoor held a quill in his hand, poised to sign. We'd arrived just in the nick of time. (What the heck is a nick anyway?)

The monarchs' table sat in the open area in the center of the room, between the two raised sets of bleacherlike seats that were filled with patrons. Knights of Crystallia stood in a ring around the bottom of the floor, between the people and the rulers. They were most concentrated, I noticed, near where the Librarians sat.

She Who Cannot Be Named sat at the front of the Librarian group, pleasantly knitting an afghan.

"What is this?" King Dartmoor asked as the rest of my team piled into the room.

"The Librarians are lying to you, Father!" Rikers declared. "They tried to kidnap me!"

"Why, that's the most distressing thing I've ever heard,"

said She Who Cannot Be Named. (You know what? That name is really too hard to type all the time. From here on, I'm going to call her Swcbn.)

My companions looked at me. I wore the Truthfinder's spectacles, one eye closed to look through the single Lens. Unfortunately, Swcbn hadn't said anything that was false — she'd avoided doing so deliberately, I'm sure.

"Father," Prince Rikers said, "we can provide proof of what happened!" He waved behind him, and the two knights we'd brought with us entered, carrying the tied and gagged Fitzroy. "This is a Librarian of the Order of the Dark Oculators! He was involved in a plot to steal books from the Royal Archives —"

"Mumf mu mumfmumf," Fitzroy added.

"— which turned into a plot to kidnap me, the royal heir!" Rikers continued.

Rikers certainly did know how to get into a part. He didn't seem as much a buffoon now that he was in his element of the court.

"Lady Librarian," King Dartmoor said, turning to Swcbn.

"I'm . . . not sure what is happening," she said. Another half-truth that didn't come out as lie.

"She does, Your Majesty," I declared, stepping up. "She ordered the death of Himalaya, who is now a member of the Smedry clan."

That caused a stir.

"Lady Librarian," the king said, red-bearded face growing very stern. "Is what he says true, or is it false?"

"I'm not sure if you should be asking me, dear. It's quite —"

"Answer the question!" the king bellowed. "Have Librarians been plotting to steal and kidnap from us while these very treaty hearings have been occurring?"

The grandmotherly Librarian looked at me, and I could tell that she knew she was caught. "I think," she said, "that my team and I should be granted a short recess to discuss."

"No recess!" the king said. "Either you answer as asked, or I'm tearing this treaty in half this instant."

The elderly Librarian pursed her lips, then finally set down her knitting. "I will admit," she said, "that some *other* branches of the Librarians have been pursuing their own ends in the city. However, this is one of the main reasons we are signing this treaty — so that you can give *my* sect the authority it needs to stop the other sects from continuing this needless war!"

"And the execution of my beloved?" Folsom demanded.

"In my eyes, young man," Swcbn said, "that one is a traitor and a turncoat. How would your own laws treat someone who committed treason?"

The room fell still. Where was my grandfather? His seat at the table was noticeably empty.

"Considering this information," said King Dartmoor, "how many of you *now* vote against signing the treaty?"

Five of the twelve monarchs raised their hands.

"And I assume Smedry would still vote against the signing," Dartmoor said, "assuming he hadn't stormed out in anger. That leaves six against six. I am the deciding vote."

"Father," the prince called. "What would a hero do?"

The king hesitated. Then, embarrassingly, he looked up at me. He stared me in the eyes. Then he ripped the treaty in two.

"I find it telling," he declared to Swcbn, "that you cannot control your own people despite the importance of these talks! I find it disturbing that you would be willing to execute one of your own for joining a kingdom with which you *claim* you want to be friends. And, most of all, I find it disgusting what I nearly did. I want you

Librarians out of my kingdom by midnight. These talks are at an end."

The room exploded with sound. There were quite a number of cheers — many of these coming from the section where the Mokians, Australia included, were sitting. There were some boos, but mostly there was just a lot of excited chatter. Draulin approached from the ranks of knights, laying a hand on the king's shoulder and — in a rare moment of emotion — nodded. She actually thought that ripping up the treaty was a good idea.

Maybe that meant she'd see Bastille's help in this entire mess as validation for restoring her daughter's knighthood. I glanced about for Bastille, but she wasn't to be found. Sing tapped my arm and pointed behind. I could see Bastille in the hallway, sitting in a chair, arms wrapped around herself, shivering. She'd lost her Warrior's Lenses back when we'd been captured, and I could see that her eyes were red and puffy.

My first instinct was to go to her, but something made me hesitate. Swcbn didn't seem particularly disturbed by these events. She'd turned back to her knitting. That bothered me.

"Socrates," I whispered.

"What's that, Alcatraz?" Sing asked.

"This guy I learned about in school," I said. "He was one of those annoying types who always asked questions."

"Okay . . ." Sing said.

Something was wrong. I began asking questions that should have bothered me long before this.

Why was the most powerful Librarian in all of the Hushlands here to negotiate a treaty that the monarchs had already decided to sign?

Why wasn't she worried at being surrounded by her enemies, capable of being captured and imprisoned at a moment's notice?

Why did I feel so unsettled, as if we hadn't really won after all?

At that moment, Draulin screamed. She collapsed to the ground, holding her head. Then every Knight of Crystallia in the room dropped to the ground, crying out in pain.

"Hello, everyone!" a voice suddenly cried. I spun to find my grandfather standing behind us. "I'm back! Did I miss anything important?"

CHAPTER 21

At that moment, a lot of things happened at once.

The common people in the crowd began to scream in fear and confusion. A group of Librarian thugs pushed their way down to the floor around Swcbn, who continued to sit and knit.

King Dartmoor unsheathed his sword and turned to face the thugs. Grandpa Smedry and I tried to rush down the stairs to get to the monarchs, but were blocked by the crowds, who were trying to flee.

"Hiccupping Huffs!" Grandpa Smedry cursed.

"Follow me, Lord Smedry!" Sing said, muscling up to the top of the stairs beside us. Then he tripped.

Now, I don't know how *you'd* react if a three-hundred-pound Mokian tripped and began to roll down the stairs toward you, but I safely say that I'd either:

1) Scream like a girl and jump out of the way.

2) Scream like a gerbil and jump out of the way.

3) Scream like a Smedry and jump out of the way.

The people on the steps chose to scream like a bunch of people on some steps, but they *did* get out of the way.

Grandpa Smedry, Folsom, Himalaya, and I charged down the stairs behind the Mokian. Prince Rikers stayed behind, looking confused. "This part actually looks dangerous," he called. "Maybe I should stay here. You know, and guard the exit."

Whatever, I thought. His father, at least, proved to have a spine. King Dartmoor stood over the body of his fallen wife, facing down the group of Librarian thugs, sword held before him. The other monarchs were in the processes of scattering away.

It looked as if the Librarians would easily cut down the king before we could reach him.

"Hey!" a voice yelled suddenly. I recognized my aunt Patty standing in the audience, pointing. As always, her voice managed to carry over any and every bit of competition. "I don't mean to be rude," she bellowed, "but is that *toilet paper* stuck to your leg?"

The Librarian thug at the front immediately looked down, then blushed, realizing that he did indeed have toilet paper stuck to him. He bent down to pull it off, causing the others to bunch up behind him awkwardly.

That distraction gave us just enough time to cover the distance to the king. Grandpa Smedry whipped out a pair of Lenses. I recognized the green specks in the glass, marking them as Windstormer's Lenses. Sure enough, the Lenses released a blast of air, knocking back the Librarians as they tried to rush the king.

"What happened to the knights?" the king yelled, desperate.

"Librarians must have corrupted the Mindstone, Brig," Grandpa Smedry said.

That's the problem with having a magic rock that connects the minds of all of your best soldiers. Take down the stone, and you take down your soldiers. Kind of like how taking out one cell phone tower can knock out the texting ability of an entire school's worth of teenage girls.

Grandpa Smedry focused on blasting the Librarians with his Lenses, but they got smart quickly. They spread out, forcing their way around the perimeter of the floor, trying to get at the king. Grandpa Smedry couldn't focus on all the different groups; there were too many.

The room was a chaotic mess. People screaming, Librarians pulling out swords, wind blowing. The monarchs were trying to escape, but the stairs were clogged again. Sing sat dazed from his roll down the stairs. He wouldn't be able to help again anytime soon.

"Alcatraz, get those monarchs out!" Grandpa Smedry said, pointing toward the wall. "Folsom, if you'd help me . . ."

And with that, Grandpa Smedry began to sing.

I stared at him, dumbfounded, until I realized this gave Folsom the music he needed to dance. Both Folsom and Himalaya spun toward the Librarians, knocking down those who had tried to push around the outsides of the room.

I turned and dashed up a section of bleacherlike seats. "Monarchs, up here!" I said. The seats here were empty, their occupants all trying to crowd out the other door.

Several of the monarchs turned toward me as I reached the far wall. I placed two hands against it and blasted it with breaking power. The entire wall fell away as if it had been shoved by the hand of a giant.

Monarchs rushed up the steps, wearing a variety of costumes and crowns: A man with dark skin in red African-style clothing. The Mokian king in his islander wrap. A king and queen in standard crowns and European robes. I counted them off, but didn't see Bastille's father.

That was, apparently, because he was still down below. I could see that he was trying to pull Draulin to safety — unfortunately, she weighed like a bazillion pounds with all that armor on, not to mention the awkward sword strapped to her back. The king must have come to the same conclusion, as he pulled free her sword and tossed it aside, then began to work off the armor.

I moved to go help, but the crowds had seen my new exit and were swarming around me. I had to fight against them, and it really slowed me down.

"Grandpa!" I yelled, pointing.

Below, my grandfather turned toward the king, then cursed. Folsom and Himalaya were holding off the Librarians pretty well, so Grandpa Smedry rushed over to help the High King. I tried to do likewise, but it was slow going with the crowd in my way. Fortunately, it looked like I wouldn't be needed.

People escaped out of the broken hole in the wall. Folsom and Himalaya handled the Librarians. My grandfather helped the High King pick up Draulin. Everything seemed good.

Swcbn continued to knit quietly.

Questions. They still itched at me.

How exactly, I wondered, *did the Librarians get to the Crystin Mindstone? That thing must be freakishly well guarded.*

Why was Swcbn acting so content? Who *had* blown up the *Hawkwind*? It had to have been someone who would have been able to get Detonator's Glass into Draulin's pack. Hers was the room that had exploded.

I glanced at Himalaya, who fought beside her new husband, knocking down enemy after enemy as my grandfather sang opera. It occurred to me that perhaps we'd overlooked something. And at that moment, I asked the most important question of all.

If there could be such a thing as a good Librarian, might there also be such a thing as an evil Knight of Crystallia? A knight who could get to the Mindstone and corrupt it? A knight who could slip a bomb into Draulin's pack? A knight who had been involved in sending Bastille out to fail?

A knight whom I had personally seen hanging around the Royal Archives within a few hours of the swap?

"Oh, no . . ." I whispered.

At that moment, one of the "unconscious" knights near Grandpa Smedry began to move. He lifted his head, and I could see a deadly smile on it. Archedis, otherwise known as Mr. Big Chin, supposedly the most accomplished of all the Knights of Crystallia.

I should have listened more to Socrates.

"Grandfather!" I screamed, trying to fight the crowd and run forward, but they were so frightened that I barely got a few steps before being pushed back again.

Grandpa Smedry turned, still singing, looking up at me and smiling. In a flash, Archedis rose, pulling free his crystalline sword. He slammed the pommel against Grandpa Smedry's head.

The old man went cross-eyed — his Talent unable to protect him from the power of a Crystin blade — and he fell to the side. With his singing gone, Himalaya and Folsom immediately stopped fighting and froze in place.

The Librarians tackled them.

I struggled against the flow of people again, trying desperately to get down. The seats on the north side were now completely empty, save for Swcbn. The grandmotherly woman looked up at me, smiling. She held up the afghan she'd been knitting.

It depicted a bloody skull. Archedis turned toward King Dartmoor.

"No!" I screamed.

The corrupted knight raised his sword. Then he froze as a small, quiet figure stepped between him and the king.

Bastille. She hadn't been affected by the fall of the Mindstone . . . because the knights themselves had cut her off it.

Bastille raised her mother's sword. I don't know where she'd gotten it — I don't even know how she'd gotten into the room. She had found a pair of Warrior's Lenses, but I could see from her profile that she was still exhausted. She looked tiny before the figure of the enormous knight, with his silvery armor and heroic smile.

"Come now," Archedis said. "You can't stand against me."

Bastille didn't reply.

"I maneuvered you into obtaining knighthood," Archedis said. "You never really deserved it. That was all a ploy to kill the old Smedry."

Kill the old Smedry. . . . Of course. Bastille and I had assumed that someone had been setting *her* up to fail so that she or her mother would be disgraced. We'd completely missed that Bastille had been acting as Grandpa Smedry's bodyguard.

It hadn't been a plot against her at all. It had been a plot against my grandfather. (And, if you're wondering, no — I couldn't actually hear what they were saying down there. But someone repeated it to me later, so give me a break.) I continued to fight against the crowd, trying to get down to her. It was all happening so quickly — though pages have passed in this narrative, it had only been moments since Archedis had stood up.

I was forced to watch as Bastille raised her mother's sword. She seemed so tired, her shoulders slumping, her stance uncertain.

"I'm the best there's ever been," Archedis said. "You think you can fight me?"

Bastille looked up, and I saw something showing through her fatigue, her pain, and her sorrow. Strength.

She attacked. Crystal met crystal with a sound that was somehow more melodic than that of steel against steel. Archedis pushed Bastille back with his superior strength, laughing.

She came at him again.

Their swords met, pinging again and again. As before, Archedis rebuffed Bastille.

And she attacked again.

And again.

And again.

Each time, her sword swung a little faster. Each time, the ringing of blades was a little louder. Each time, her posture was a little more firm. She fought, refusing to be beaten down.

Archedis stopped laughing. His face grew solemn, then angry. Bastille threw herself at him repeatedly, her sword becoming a flurry of motion, the crystalline blade flashing with iridescence as it shattered light from the windows, throwing out sparkling colors.

And then Bastille actually started to push Archedis back.

Few people outside of Crystallia have seen two Crystin fight in earnest. The fleeing crowd slowed, its members turning back. Librarian thugs stopped beating on Himalaya and Folsom. Even I hesitated. We all grew still, as if in reverence, and the once chaotic room became as quiet as a concert hall.

We were an audience, watching a duet. A duet in which the violinists tried to ram their violins down each other's throats.

The massive knight and the spindly girl circled, their swords beating against each other as if in a prescribed rhythm. The weapons seemed things of beauty, the way they reflected the light. Two people trying to kill each other with rainbows.

Bastille should have lost. She was smaller, weaker, and exhausted. Yet each time Archedis threw her down, she scrambled back to her feet and attacked with even more fury and determination. To the side, her father, the king, watched in awe. To my surprise, I even saw her mother stir. The woman looked dazed and sick, but she seemed to have regained enough consciousness to open her eyes.

Archedis made a mistake. He tripped slightly against a fallen Librarian thug. It was the first error I'd seen him make, but that didn't matter. Bastille was on him in a heartbeat, pounding her sword against his, forcing him backward from his precarious position.

Looking dumbfounded, Archedis tripped backward and fell onto his armored butt. Bastille's sword froze at his neck, a hair's width from slicing his head free.

"I . . . yield," Archedis said, sounding utterly shocked.

I finally managed to shove my way through the crowd, which had been stunned by the beautiful fight. I skidded to a stop beside my grandfather. He was breathing, though unconscious. He appeared to be humming to himself in his sleep.

"Alcatraz," Bastille said.

I looked over at her. She still had her sword at Archedis's neck.

"I have something for you to do," she said, nodding to Archedis.

I smiled, then walked over to the fallen knight.

"Look, hey," he said, smiling. "I'm a double agent, really. I was just trying to infiltrate them. I . . . uh, is it true that you have a Truthfinder's Lens?"

I nodded.

"Oh," he said, knowing that I'd been able to see that he was lying.

"Do it," Bastille said, nodding toward the ground.

"Gladly," I said, reaching down to touch Archedis's blade. With a magnificent crackling sound, it shattered beneath the power of my Talent.

Swcbn finally put down her knitting. "You," she said, "are very *bad* children. No cookies for you."

And with that, she vanished — replaced with an exact statue of herself, sitting in that very position.

ROYAL EPILOGUE (*Not* a Chapter)

THERE COMES A TIME IN EVERY BOOK WHEN A SINGLE, IMPORTANT QUESTION MUST BE ASKED: "WHERE'S MY LUNCH?"

THAT TIME ISN'T RIGHT NOW. HOWEVER, IT IS TIME TO ASK ANOTHER QUESTION, ALMOST AS IMPORTANT: "SO, WHAT'S THE POINT?"

IT'S AN EXCELLENT QUESTION. WE SHOULD ASK IT ABOUT EVERYTHING WE READ. THE PROBLEM IS, I HAVE NO IDEA HOW TO ANSWER IT.

THE POINT OF THIS BOOK IS REALLY UP TO YOU. MY POINT IN WRITING IT WAS TO LOOK AT MY LIFE, TO EXPOSE IT, TO ILLUMINATE IT. AS SOCRATES ONCE SAID, "THE UNEXAMINED LIFE IS NOT WORTH LIVING."

HE DIED FOR TEACHING THAT TO PEOPLE. I FEEL I SHOULD HAVE DIED YEARS AGO. INSTEAD, I PROVED MYSELF TO BE A COWARD. YOU'LL SEE WHAT I MEAN, EVENTUALLY.

THIS BOOK MEANS WHATEVER YOU MAKE OF IT. FOR SOME, IT WILL BE ABOUT THE DANGERS OF FAME. FOR OTHERS, IT WILL BE ABOUT TURNING YOUR FLAWS INTO TALENTS. FOR MANY, IT WILL SIMPLY BE ENTERTAINMENT, WHICH IS REALLY QUITE ALL RIGHT. YET FOR OTHERS, IT WILL BE ABOUT LEARNING TO QUESTION EVERYTHING, EVEN THAT WHICH YOU BELIEVE.

FOR, YOU SEE, THE MOST IMPORTANT TRUTHS CAN ALWAYS WITHSTAND A LITTLE EXAMINATION.

ONE WEEK AFTER THE DEFEAT OF ARCHEDIS AND THE LIBRARIANS, I SAT IN THE CHAMBER OF KINGS. GRANDPA SMEDRY SAT TO MY LEFT, DRESSED IN HIS FINEST TUXEDO. BASTILLE SAT TO MY RIGHT, WEARING

THE PLATE ARMOR OF A FULL KNIGHT OF CRYSTALLIA. (YES, OF COURSE SHE GOT HER KNIGHTHOOD BACK. AS IF THE KNIGHTS COULD REFUSE AFTER WATCHING HER DEFEAT ARCHEDIS WHILE THEY LAY ON THE GROUND DROOLING.)

I STILL WASN'T CLEAR ON WHAT ARCHEDIS HAD DONE. FROM WHAT I GATHER, THE MINDSTONE WAS CUT FROM THE SPIRE OF THE WORLD ITSELF. LIKE THE SPIRE, THE MINDSTONE HAS THE POWER TO RADIATE ENERGY AND KNOWLEDGE TO EVERYONE CONNECTED TO IT. ARCHEDIS HAD BEEN ABLE TO RESIST THE SUNDERING AS HE'D CUT HIMSELF OFF FROM THE MINDSTONE EARLIER.

EITHER WAY, WITH BOTH BASTILLE AND ARCHEDIS BEING CUT OFF — AND WITH BOTH WEARING WARRIOR'S LENSES — THEIR SPEED AND STRENGTH HAD BEEN EQUALIZED. AND BASTILLE HAD BEATEN HIM. SHE'D WON BECAUSE OF HER SKILL AND HER TENACITY, WHICH I'D SAY ARE THE MORE IMPORTANT INDICATORS OF KNIGHTHOOD. SHE'D WORN HER SILVERY ARMOR VIRTUALLY NONSTOP SINCE IT HAD BEEN GIVEN BACK TO HER. A CRYSTAL SWORD HUNG FROM HER BACK, NEWLY BONDED TO BASTILLE.

"CAN'T WE GET ON WITH THIS?" SHE SNAPPED. "SHATTERING GLASS, SMEDRY. YOUR FATHER IS SUCH A DRAMA HOG."

I SMILED. THAT WAS ANOTHER SIGN SHE WAS FEELING BETTER — SHE WAS BACK TO HER USUAL CHARMING SELF.

"WHAT'S WRONG WITH YOU?" SHE SAID, EYEING ME. "STOP STARING AT ME."

"I'M NOT STARING AT YOU," I SAID. "I'M HAVING AN INTERNAL MONO-LOGUE TO CATCH THE READERS UP ON WHAT HAS HAPPENED SINCE THE LAST CHAPTER. IT'S CALLED A DENOUEMENT."

SHE ROLLED HER EYES. "THEN WE CAN'T ACTUALLY BE HAVING THIS CONVERSATION; IT'S SOMETHING YOU JUST INSERTED INTO THE TEXT WHILE WRITING THE BOOK YEARS LATER. IT'S A LITERARY DEVICE — THE CON-VERSATION DIDN'T EXIST."

"OH, RIGHT," I SAID.

"YOU'RE SUCH A FREAK."

FREAK OR NOT, I WAS HAPPY. YES, MY MOTHER ESCAPED WITH THE BOOK. YES, SWCBN ESCAPED AS WELL. BUT WE CAUGHT ARCHEDIS, SAVED MOKIA, AND GOT BACK MY FATHER'S PAIR OF TRANSLATOR'S LENSES.

I'D SHOWN THEM TO HIM. HE'D BEEN SURPRISED, HAD TAKEN THEM BACK, THEN HAD RETURNED TO WHATEVER IMPORTANT "WORK" IT WAS HE'D BEEN DOING THIS WHOLE TIME. WE WERE SUPPOSED TO FIND OUT ABOUT IT TODAY; HE WAS GOING TO PRESENT HIS FINDINGS BEFORE THE MONARCHS. APPARENTLY, HE ALWAYS REVEALED HIS DISCOVERIES THIS WAY.

SO — OF COURSE — THE PLACE WAS A CIRCUS. NO, LITERALLY. THERE WAS A CIRCUS OUTSIDE THE FRONT OF THE PALACE TO ENTER-TAIN THE KIDS WHILE THEIR PARENTS CAME IN TO LISTEN TO MY FATHER'S GRAND SPEECH. THE PLACE WAS ALMOST AS PACKED AS IT HAD BEEN DURING THE TREATY RATIFICATION.

Hopefully, this time there would be fewer Librarian hijinks. (Those wacky Librarians and their hijinks.)

There was a large number of reporter types waiting in the reaches of the room, anticipating my father's announcement. As I'd come to learn, anything involving the Smedry family was news to the Free Kingdomers. This news, however, was even more important.

The last time my father had held a session like this, he'd announced that he had discovered a way to collect the Sands of Rashid. The time before that, he'd explained that he'd broken the secret of Transporter's Glass. People were expecting a lot from this speech.

I couldn't help but feel that it was all just a little . . . bad for my father's ego. I mean, a *circus*? Who gets a circus thrown for them?

I glanced at Bastille. "You dealt with this kind of stuff most of your childhood, didn't you?"

"This kind of stuff?" she asked.

"Fame. Notoriety. People paying attention to everything you do."

She nodded.

"So how did you deal with it?" I asked. "And not let it ruin you?"

"How do you know it *didn't* ruin me?" she asked. "Aren't princesses supposed to be nice and sweet and stuff like that? Wear pink dresses and tiaras?"

"Well . . ."

"Pink dresses," Bastille said, her eyes narrowing. "Someone gave me a pink dress once. I burned it."

Ah, I thought. That's right; I forgot. Bastille got around fame's touch by being a freaking psychopath.

"You'll learn, lad," Grandpa Smedry said from beside me. "It might take some time, but you'll figure it out."

"My father never did," I said.

Grandpa Smedry hesitated. "Oh, well, I don't know about that. I think he did, for a while. Back around the time he got married. I just think he forgot."

Around the time he got married. The words made me think of Folsom and Himalaya. We'd saved them seats, but they were late. As I looked around, I caught a glance of them working their way through the crowd. Grandpa Smedry waved enthusiastically, though they'd obviously already seen us.

But, then, that's Grandpa.

"Sorry," Folsom said as he and his new wife seated themselves. "Getting some last-minute packing done."

"You still determined to go through with this?" Grandpa Smedry asked.

Himalaya nodded. "We're moving to the Hushlands. I think . . . well, there isn't much I can do for my fellow Librarians here."

"We'll start an underground resistance for good Librarians," Folsom said.

"Lybrarians," Himalaya said. "I've already begun working on a pamphlet!"

She pulled out a sheet of paper. Ten Steps to Being Less Evil, it read. A Helpful Guide for Those Who Want to Take the "Lie" out of "Liebrarian."

"That's . . . just great," I said. I wasn't certain how else to respond. Fortunately for me, my father chose that moment to make his entrance — which was particularly good, since this scene was starting to feel a little long anyway.

The monarchs sat behind a long table facing a raised podium. We all grew quiet as my father approached, wearing dark robes to mark him as a scientist. The crowd hushed.

"As you may have heard," he said, his voice carrying through the room, "I have recently returned from the Library of Alexandria. I spent some time as a Curator, escaping their clutches with my soul intact by the means of clever planning."

"YEAH," BASTILLE MUTTERED, "CLEVER PLANNING, AND SOME UNDE-
SERVED HELP." SING, WHO SAT IN FRONT OF US, GAVE HER A
DISAPPROVING LOOK.

"THE PURPOSE OF ALL THIS," MY FATHER CONTINUED, "WAS
TO GAIN ACCESS TO THE FABLED TEXTS COLLECTED AND CONTROLLED
BY THE CURATORS OF ALEXANDRIA. HAVING MANAGED TO CRE-
ATE A PAIR OF TRANSLATOR'S LENSES FROM THE SANDS OF RASHID —"

THIS CAUSED A RIPPLE OF DISCUSSION IN THE CROWD.

"— I WAS ABLE TO READ TEXTS IN THE FORGOTTEN LANGUAGE," MY
FATHER CONTINUED. "I WAS TAKEN BY THE CURATORS AND TRANS-
FORMED INTO ONE OF THEM, BUT STILL RETAINED ENOUGH FREE WILL TO
SNEAK THE LENSES FROM MY POSSESSIONS AND USE THEM TO READ. THIS
ALLOWED ME TO SPEND WEEKS STUDYING THE MOST VALUABLE CONTENTS
OF THE LIBRARY."

HE STOPPED, LEANING FORWARD ON THE PODIUM, SMILING WINNINGLY.
HE CERTAINLY DID HAVE A CHARM ABOUT HIM, WHEN HE WANTED TO
IMPRESS PEOPLE.

IN THAT MOMENT, LOOKING AT THAT SMILE, I COULD SWEAR THAT
I'D SEEN HIM SOMEWHERE, LONG BEFORE MY VISIT TO THE LIBRARY OF
ALEXANDRIA.

"WHAT I DID," MY FATHER CONTINUED, "WAS DANGEROUS; SOME MAY
EVEN CALL IT BRASH. I COULDN'T KNOW THAT I'D HAVE ENOUGH FREE-
DOM AS A CURATOR TO STUDY THE TEXTS, NOR COULD I COUNT ON THE

FACT THAT I'D BE ABLE TO USE MY LENSES TO READ THE FORGOTTEN LANGUAGE."

HE PAUSED FOR DRAMATIC EFFECT. "BUT I DID IT ANYWAY. FOR THAT IS THE SMEDRY WAY."

"HE STOLE THAT LINE FROM ME, BY THE WAY," GRANDPA SMEDRY WHISPERED TO US.

MY FATHER CONTINUED. "I'VE SPENT THE LAST TWO WEEKS WRITING DOWN THE THINGS I MEMORIZED WHILE I WAS A CURATOR. SECRETS LOST IN TIME, MYSTERIES KNOWN ONLY TO THE INCARNA. I'VE ANALYZED THEM, AND AM THE ONLY MAN TO READ AND UNDERSTAND THEIR WORKS FOR OVER TWO MILLENNIA."

HE LOOKED OVER THE CROWD. "THROUGH THIS," HE SAID, "I HAVE DISCOVERED THE METHOD BY WHICH THE SMEDRY TALENTS WERE CREATED AND GIVEN TO MY FAMILY."

WHAT? I THOUGHT, SHOCKED.

"IMPOSSIBLE," BASTILLE SAID, AND THE CROWD AROUND US BEGAN TO SPEAK ANIMATEDLY.

I GLANCED AT MY GRANDFATHER. THOUGH THE OLD MAN IS USUALLY WACKIER THAN A PENGUIN-WRANGLING EXPEDITION TO FLORIDA, OCCASIONALLY I CATCH A HINT OF WISDOM IN HIS FACE. HE HAS A DEPTH THAT HE DOESN'T OFTEN SHOW.

HE TURNED TOWARD ME, MEETING MY EYES, AND I COULD TELL THAT HE WAS WORRIED. VERY WORRIED.

"I ANTICIPATE GREAT THINGS FROM THIS," MY FATHER SAID, HUSHING THE CROWD. "WITH A LITTLE MORE RESEARCH, I BELIEVE I CAN DISCOVER HOW TO GIVE TALENTS TO ORDINARY PEOPLE. I IMAGINE A WORLD, NOT SO DISTANT IN THE FUTURE, WHERE EVERYONE HAS A SMEDRY TALENT."

AND THEN HE WAS DONE. HE RETREATED FROM THE PODIUM, STEPPING DOWN TO SPEAK WITH THE MONARCHS. THE ROOM, OF COURSE, GREW LOUD WITH DISCUSSIONS. I FOUND MYSELF STANDING, PUSHING MY WAY DOWN TO THE FLOOR OF THE ROOM. I APPROACHED THE MONARCHS, AND THE KNIGHTS STANDING GUARD THERE LET ME PASS.

". . . NEED ACCESS TO THE ROYAL ARCHIVES," MY FATHER WAS SAYING TO THE MONARCHS.

"NOT A LIBRARY," I FOUND MYSELF WHISPERING.

MY FATHER DIDN'T NOTICE ME. "THERE ARE SOME BOOKS THERE I BELIEVE WOULD BE OF USE TO MY INVESTIGATIONS, NOW THAT I'VE RECOVERED MY TRANSLATOR'S LENSES. ONE VOLUME, IN PARTICULAR, WAS CONSPICUOUSLY MISSING FROM THE LIBRARY OF ALEXANDRIA — THE CURATORS CLAIMED THEIR COPY HAD BEEN BURNED IN A VERY STRANGE ACCIDENT. FORTUNATELY, I BELIEVE THERE MAY BE ANOTHER ONE HERE."

"IT'S GONE," I SAID, MY VOICE SOFT IN THE ROOM'S BUZZING VOICES.

ATTICA TURNED TO ME, AS DID SEVERAL OF THE MONARCHS. "WHAT IS THAT, SON?" MY FATHER ASKED.

"DIDN'T YOU PAY ATTENTION AT ALL TO WHAT HAPPENED LAST WEEK?" I DEMANDED. "MOTHER HAS THE BOOK. THE ONE YOU WANT. SHE STOLE IT FROM THE ARCHIVES."

MY FATHER HESITATED, THEN NODDED TO THE MONARCHS. "EXCUSE US." HE PULLED ME ASIDE. "NOW, WHAT IS THIS?"

"SHE STOLE IT," I SAID. "THE BOOK YOU WANT, THE ONE WRITTEN BY THE SCRIBE OF ALCATRAZ THE FIRST. SHE TOOK IT FROM THE ARCHIVES. THAT'S WHAT THE *ENTIRE MESS LAST WEEK* WAS ABOUT!"

"I THOUGHT THAT WAS AN ASSASSINATION ATTEMPT ON THE MONARCHS," HE SAID.

"THAT WAS ONLY PART OF IT. I SENT YOU A MESSAGE IN THE MIDDLE OF IT, ASKING YOU TO COME HELP US PROTECT THE ARCHIVES, BUT YOU COMPLETELY IGNORED IT!"

HE WAVED AN INDIFFERENT HAND. "I WAS OCCUPIED WITH GREATER THINGS. YOU MUST BE MISTAKEN — I'LL LOOK THROUGH THE ARCHIVES AND —"

"I LOOKED ALREADY," I SAID. "I'VE LOOKED AT THE TITLE OF EVERY SINGLE BOOK IN THERE THAT WAS WRITTEN IN THE FORGOTTEN LANGUAGE. THEY'RE ALL COOKBOOKS OR LEDGERS OR THINGS. EXCEPT THAT ONE MY MOTHER TOOK."

"AND YOU LET HER STEAL IT?" MY FATHER DEMANDED INDIGNANTLY.

LET HER. I TOOK A DEEP BREATH. (AND, NEXT TIME YOU THINK YOUR

PARENTS ARE FRUSTRATING, MIGHT I INVITE YOU TO READ THIS PASSAGE THROUGH ONE MORE TIME?)

"I BELIEVE," A NEW VOICE SAID, "THAT YOUNG ALCATRAZ DID EVERY-THING HE COULD TO STOP THE AFOREMENTIONED THEFT."

MY FATHER TURNED TO SEE KING DARTMOOR, WEARING HIS CROWN AND BLUE-GOLD ROBES, STANDING BEHIND HIM. THE KING NODDED TO ME. "PRINCE RIKERS HAS SPOKEN AT LENGTH OF THE EVENT, ATTICA. I BELIEVE THERE WILL BE A NOVEL FORTHCOMING."

WONDERFUL, I THOUGHT.

"WELL," MY FATHER SAID, "I GUESS ... WELL, THIS CHANGES EVERYTHING. ..."

"WHAT IS THIS ABOUT GIVING EVERYONE TALENTS, ATTICA?" THE KING ASKED. "IS THAT REALLY WISE? FROM WHAT I HEAR, SMEDRY TALENTS CAN BE VERY UNPREDICTABLE."

"WE CAN CONTROL THEM," MY FATHER SAID, WAVING ANOTHER INDIF-FERENT HAND. "YOU KNOW HOW THE PEOPLE DREAM OF HAVING OUR POWERS. WELL, I WILL BE THE ONE TO MAKE THOSE DREAMS BECOME A REALITY."

SO THAT WAS WHAT IT WAS ABOUT. MY FATHER, SEALING HIS LEG-ACY. BEING THE HERO WHO MADE EVERYONE CAPABLE OF HAVING A TALENT.

BUT IF EVERYONE HAD A SMEDRY TALENT ... THEN, WELL, WHAT WOULD THAT MEAN FOR US? WE WOULDN'T BE THE ONLY ONES WITH TALENTS ANYMORE. THAT MADE ME FEEL A LITTLE SICK.

YES, I KNOW IT IS SELFISH, BUT THAT'S HOW I FELT. I THINK THIS IS — PERHAPS — THE CAPSTONE OF THIS BOOK. AFTER ALL I'D BEEN THROUGH, AFTER ALL THE FIGHTING TO HELP THE FREE KINGDOMS, I WAS STILL SELFISH ENOUGH TO WANT TO KEEP THE TALENTS FOR MYSELF.

BECAUSE THE TALENTS WERE WHAT MADE US SPECIAL, WEREN'T THEY?

"I WILL HAVE TO THINK ON THIS MORE," MY FATHER SAID. "IT APPEARS THAT WE'LL HAVE TO SEARCH OUT THAT BOOK. EVEN IF IT MEANS CONFRONTING . . . HER."

HE NODDED TO THE KINGS, THEN WALKED AWAY. HE PUT ON A SMIL-ING FACE WHEN HE MET WITH THE PRESS, BUT I COULD TELL THAT HE WAS BOTHERED. THE DISAPPEARANCE OF THAT BOOK HAD FOULED UP HIS PLANS.

WELL, I THOUGHT, HE SHOULD HAVE PAID BETTER ATTENTION!

I KNEW IT WAS SILLY, BUT I COULDN'T HELP FEELING THAT I'D LET HIM DOWN. THAT THIS WAS MY FAULT. I TRIED TO SHAKE MYSELF OUT OF IT AND WALKED BACK TO MY GRANDFATHER AND THE OTHERS.

HAD MY PARENTS BEEN LIKE FOLSOM AND HIMALAYA ONCE? BRIGHT, LOVING, FULL OF EXCITEMENT? IF SO, WHAT HAD GONE WRONG? HIMALAYA WAS A LIBRARIAN AND FOLSOM WAS A SMEDRY. WERE THEY DOOMED TO THE SAME FATE AS MY PARENTS?

AND SMEDRY TALENTS FOR EVERYONE. MY MIND DRIFTED BACK TO THE WORDS I'D READ ON THE WALL OF THE TOMB OF ALCATRAZ THE FIRST.

OUR DESIRES HAVE BROUGHT US LOW. WE SOUGHT TO TOUCH THE POWERS OF ETERNITY, THEN DRAW THEM DOWN UPON OURSELVES. BUT WE BROUGHT WITH THEM SOMETHING WE DID NOT INTEND. . . .

THE BANE OF INCARNA. THAT WHICH TWISTS, THAT WHICH COR-RUPTS, AND THAT WHICH DESTROYS.

THE DARK TALENT.

WHEREVER MY FATHER WENT ON HIS QUEST TO DISCOVER HOW TO "MAKE" SMEDRY TALENTS, I DETERMINED THAT I WOULD FOLLOW AFTER HIM. I WOULD WATCH, AND MAKE CERTAIN HE DIDN'T DO ANY-THING TOO RASH.

I HAD TO BE READY TO STOP HIM, IF NEED BE.

THE LAST PAGES

ALCATRAZ WALKS ONTO THE STAGE. HE SMILES AT THE AUDIENCE, LOOKING RIGHT INTO THE CAMERA.

"HELLO," HE SAYS. "AND WELCOME TO THE AFTER-BOOK SPECIAL. I'M YOUR HOST, ALCATRAZ SMEDRY."

"AND I'M BASTILLE DARTMOOR," BASTILLE SAYS, JOINING ALCATRAZ ON THE STAGE.

ALCATRAZ NODS. "WE'RE HERE TO TALK TO YOU ABOUT A PERNICIOUS EVIL THAT IS PLAGUING TODAY'S YOUTH. A TERRIBLE, AWFUL HABIT THAT IS DESTROYING THEM FROM THE INSIDE OUT."

BASTILLE LOOKS AT THE CAMERA. "HE'S TALKING, OF COURSE, ABOUT SKIPPING TO THE ENDS OF BOOKS AND READING THE LAST PAGES FIRST."

"WE CALL IT 'LAST-PAGING,'" ALCATRAZ SAYS. "YOU MAY THINK IT DOESN'T INVOLVE YOU OR YOUR FRIENDS, BUT STUDIES SHOW THAT THERE HAS BEEN A 4,000.024 PERCENT INCREASE IN LAST-PAGING DURING THE PAST SEVEN MINUTES ALONE."

"THAT'S RIGHT, ALCATRAZ," BASTILLE SAYS. "AND DID YOU KNOW THAT LAST-PAGING IS THE LARGEST CAUSE OF CANCER IN DOMESTICATED FRUIT BATS?"

"REALLY?"

"YES INDEED. ALSO, LAST-PAGING MAKES YOU LOSE SLEEP, GROW HAIR IN FUNNY PLACES, AND CAN DECREASE YOUR ABILITY TO PLAY HALO BY FORTY-FIVE PERCENT."

"WOW," ALCATRAZ SAYS. "WHY WOULD ANYONE DO IT?"

"WE'RE NOT CERTAIN. WE ONLY KNOW THAT IT HAPPENS, AND THAT THIS TERRIBLE DISEASE ISN'T FULLY UNDERSTOOD. FORTUNATELY, WE'VE TAKEN ACTIONS TO COMBAT IT."

"SUCH AS PUTTING TERRIBLE AFTER-BOOK SPECIALS AT THE BACKS OF BOOKS TO MAKE PEOPLE FEEL SICK?" ALCATRAZ ASKS HELPFULLY.

"THAT'S RIGHT," BASTILLE SAYS. "STAY AWAY FROM LAST-PAGING, KIDS! REMEMBER, THE MORE YOU KNOW . . ."

". . . THE MORE YOU CAN FORGET TOMORROW!" ALCATRAZ SAYS. "GOOD NIGHT, FOLKS. AND BE SURE TO JOIN US FOR NEXT WEEK'S AFTER-BOOK SPECIAL, WHERE WE EXPOSE THE DANGERS OF GERBIL SNORTING!"

AUTHOR'S AFTERWORD

No, we're not done yet. Be patient. We've only had three endings so far; we can stand another one. Both of my other books had afterwords, so this one will too. (And if we need to send someone to Valinor to justify this last ending, let me know. I'm not going to marry Rosie, though.)

Anyway, there you have it. My first visit to Nalhalla, my first experience with fame. You've seen the actions of a hero and the actions of a fool — and you know that both hero and fool are the same person.

I know I said that this was the book where you'd see me fail — and, in a way, I did fail. I let my mother escape with the Incarna text. However, I realize this wasn't as big a failure as you might have been expecting.

You should have known. I won't warn you when my big failure is about to arrive. It will hurt far more when it's a surprise.

You'll see.

About the Author

Brandon Sanderson is the second-leading cause of cancer in domesticated fruit bats. He didn't write this book; Alcatraz Smedry did. However, as Brandon's name is synonymous with *Elantris*, the Mistborn series, and other "big, boring fantasy books nobody wants to read," Alcatraz figured it would be a good name to put on this book. It might help keep the Librarians from discovering what's really in here.

Brandon Sanderson is known to be one of those annoying people who always answers questions with other questions. You want to know why? Why does it matter? What do you hope to learn? Why would you want to know more about him? Don't you realize that he's a very silly person?

The end. (Finally.)

Acknowledgments

I want to thank my awesome agent, Joshua Bilmes, for being, well, awesome. Thanks also to my editor at Scholastic, Jennifer Rees, whose pleasant personality and editorial know-how make the process of publishing a book so much easier. Peter and Karen Ahlstrom were kind enough to read the manuscript and give me excellent suggestions. Janci Patterson also gave me feedback that was very valuable, even though her comments were written in glaring pink ink! I'd like to thank my lovely wife, Emily Sanderson, who helped with this book in ways too numerous to list here. Finally, a special thank-you goes to Mrs. Bushman's sixth-grade students (you know who you are!) who have been so enthusiastic about my books.

— Brandon Sanderson